Culinary Confessions

Joanne Lambo

Contents

Chapter 1

Here Comes the Bride (Zilla)

Present Day – Monday, May 27, 2019

Baking is the result of hard work, love and creativity all rolled into one. Maddie's thoughts drifted to this quote as she sifted the flour, sugar, and salt into a large bowl. She used her elbow to play the video on her phone, listening as the woman directed her on how to make her famous chocolate cupcakes. Maddie smiled, feeling the stress she had earlier begin to melt away. Whenever the brunette was stressed about anything, baking provided a temporary comfort. She loved the way her creativity seemed to flow out of that activity. She fiddled with the whisk in her hand, sifting the salt along with the cocoa powder.

She had been stressed about her English assignment, even though it seemed simple at first. She had to answer two questions about the story that had been read over the weekend. She had the story over and over, but still could not manage to answer those questions in a way that made sense to her. Maddie found herself looking outside the window, listening to the chirping of the

1

birds. *Focus, Maddie! You cannot afford to mess up this recipe.*

She shared a room with her younger sister, Mia, who was busy playing Portal upstairs.

"Maddie, can you come here for a second?" their mom called out from upstairs.

Maddie took a deep breath. Any time she was stressed about something, her anxiety flared up. This was one of those moments. Anxiety was like a current stream of thoughts that floated around in the brain, desperately wishing to come out. It wasn't a good feeling, that was for sure. What happened in real life was contrary to she had imagined as a worst case scenario: their mom or dad usually asked her to help with something, then she would go back to whatever she was preoccupied with. Even she didn't do anything wrong, she found herself on edge at times.

She quickly texted Mia, asking her if she could help their mom out instead. Mia's smooth, bronze skin was the only thing that separated the two girls from each other and the fact that Maddie was four years older than her. Mia had inherited their mom's long, black hair that went all the way to the top of her shoulders. While they had their differences, it didn't change the tight-knit bond they had with one another. Whenever Maddie found her anxiety flaring up, Mia often helped to calm her down, making her laugh by showing her funny videos or just being there for her in general. A *ding* from her phone indicated that Mia had responded to her text. *She called you, not me. So get your butt on over there and go see what she wants.* She ended the text with a laughing emoji, causing Maddie to smile.

She hoped that their mom would not take very long. She needed to finish baking, then get back to finishing her essay. If she didn't finish the thing before Wednesday, it would be a *lot* harder to get someone to look it over. The twenty-one-year-old was majoring in Graphic Design, but for one reason or another, Lakeview University required that she take classes not related to her major. She laid the whisk down, hoping that whatever news her mom had for her would be something exciting.

Maddie passed by the living room where her dad was hard at work on his laptop. Her light-brown skin was a byproduct of the love their parents had for one another. Even though she was confident in her looks, it was her dad's sense of humor and her mom's undeterred faith that she coveted. She had faith, but often wished that her father's sense of humor were hereditary, since humor often helped to put her mind at ease. Like all parents, they had their flaws, but she soon learned to accept them, just like they did for her.

She took a deep breath, something her dad was quick to notice.

"Everything okay?" he asked. Her father had a comforting aura about him, which she was thankful for when she was up to her knees in homework assignments. "Your mom just called you."

She looked up at him. "Yeah," she said, before shifting her weight from one foot to another.

Her dad looked over to her, getting up to ruffle his daughter's hair. "I'm sure everything's fine. Who knows? It might even be something good."

"Thanks, Dad," she said, giving him a kiss on the cheek.

"What are you up to?" he asked.

Maddie grinned. He probably heard her whisking something in the kitchen. "Making chocolate cupcakes."

Her dad laughed. "I thought you learned from the last dessert you made."

She averted her gaze somewhere else, feeling her cheeks getting warm. The carrot cake incident was probably one of the worst dessert recipes she ever made. The recipe had looked right when she started out with it, but combine getting distracted by her cat and, well... "I got distracted by our cat, Clara, you know that." She perked her head up. "Besides, this one will be better, you'll see."

Her dad chuckled, knowing he was never going to talk his daughter out of this. His nose then scrunched up in disgust at the mention of her cat. "You're all delusional in loving that pest."

Maddie stuck her nose in the air. "Hmph!" She ran up the stairs and into her parents' bedroom, where her mom was busy on the phone.

She and her mother were both a height of five feet and four inches tall, with her mother carrying it in stride. Her mother worked as a public middle school teacher at Lakeview High, having a no-nonsense attitude that made many respect, or resent her with no in-between.

Her mother, Aria, had pressed the mute button on the phone, motioning for Maddie to come forward. "Good morning Maddie. Did you sleep well?"

Maddie nodded. She walked over to her mom's side, giving her a tight hug. Hugs always managed to make her feel a little better, no matter what mood she was in. "Who are you talking to?" she asked, her curiosity peaking.

Aria continued. "I'm just got off the phone with a family friend of ours. She said that she's never seen Justin's face light up like that before. It must be from you talking to him."

Maddie felt a smile begin to form from the corners of her mouth at the mention of his name. She and Justin had been through thick and thin ever since high school. They had been video chatting every weekend, with one call, in particular, being the day she had confided in him the reason why her mom put her in private school, but never went into specifics for fear of being judged.

Her mother continued. "Well, he has an aunt named Caroline who lives here in Atlanta, and Justin referred to you, as I quote, the best baker he has ever seen."

Averting her gaze, Maddie seemed happy at how highly Justin spoke of her, even if he was among the best of the best at culinary school. *Speaking of which, he should be arriving in Atlanta by tomorrow afternoon.*

"Anyway, she wants to know if you'll agree to make a cake for her wedding and that if you do, that she'll spread the word about your business so that you can get more customers. Now, I know you have schoolwork and everything, but I trust you to get the job done. Think you're up for it?"

Struggling to come up with an answer, Maddie tried to mentally weigh the pros and cons. If she dedicated most her time to working on the cake, she would still have time to celebrate her birthday. "When does she want the cake?" she asked, her mind drifting back to her college classes, each with a given task to follow. She had to study for a quiz in both her *History Since 1500* class and English class; then, she would have to meet up with her classmates in the library next Tuesday to discuss how their presentation was going to go.

"She wants a summer wedding so probably a month from now. Say, July thirteenth?"

Smiling, Maddie began to calculate how much time the project would take. July 13th was her birthday, and, based on her research, she would have to make the cake four to five days in advance for it to taste fresh.

Aria continued. "I know your birthday is that day, Mads, so I'd understand if you'd want to turn down this offer. So, what do you say?"

She contemplated her mother's words. If she took this order, it could be good for business. She smiled, thinking of all the things she could do to add her own flair to the cake. She could use different flowers for the cake topper, what type of filling she would use. *Oh! Maybe she could use gardenias for the centerpiece...*

"Maddie?"

The brunette snapped out of her reverie. "Sorry, Mom, I was just thinking, that's all."

Aria looked at her daughter, rubbing the back of her neck. "Well, there is one other thing I should mention."

Her mom was making a big deal out of nothing. Nothing could take away the excitement of having to make her family friend's cake and for Miss Caroline of all people. She was considered to be one of the most influential people in town.

Maddie's eyes wandered around the living room, her eyes focusing on the wren chirping outside her family's house. The wren chirped at her, causing her to smile. She looked up at her mom, who had an unpleasant frown on her face.

"Maddie, focus," her mom said, getting her back to the task at hand.

She winced. "Sorry, Mom," she said, looking up at her.

Aria let out a good-natured sigh. "Anyway, the other thing I wanted to mention is that you shouldn't let Miss Caroline boss you around. I know you can handle it, but... " Her mother avoided looking her in the eyes, putting on a strained smile for her benefit.

She saw through the smile and gave her a kiss on the cheek. "Don't worry, Mom. If there's anything I can't handle, I'll be sure to ask you, my sister, or my friends for help. Just tell her that I need a bit of time to think about it first but to text me the details regarding the type of cake, the filling, the design, the cake's decoration, things like that, in the case that I change my mind."

She fiddled with her hair, her mom's words resonating with her. Her mom knew she had a habit of saying yes to anyone who needed help whether it was with an assignment or a study guide for the final exam. This time was going to be different. *She knew herself...well, kind of....*

Maddie's mother wrapped her arms around her, pulling her into a tight hug. "That's my girl." She turned away from her daughter, unmuting the call she had with her friend. "Hello, Caroline? Maddie's here, hang on." She put the phone on speaker so Maddie could hear Caroline's voice.

"Can you hear me, Dear?" Miss Caroline asked, her voice sounding loud and clear to Maddie.

"I can hear you!" she responded back.

"Okay, good! I understand if you need some more time to think about it, Dearie. You want to know all the information beforehand, am I right? I'll send the details to you tomorrow morning. Oh, and here's an extra incentive to accept the offer: if the cake exceeds my expectations, I'll make sure to refer you to all my friends, and on top of that, pay you extra. I'm excited to see what you come up with as well. Justin's told me all about your baking abilities and I must say, I'm very impressed!"

Maddie's cheeks grew red at the praise she received. "Thank you, Miss Caroline. I'll be waiting to receive all the details."

"I'll call you next Tuesday morning at 8:30 a.m. sharp to give you the details of how I want the cake to be. Bye-bye now," Miss Caroline said before hanging up.

After the call, Maddie hugged her mom once more and ran downstairs, continuing with the recipe she had started a few hours before.

* * *

Maddie laid awake in bed that night, thinking of what kind of decoration she could put on the cake itself. She loved baking and knew that if this project succeeded, it would be good for business and gain some more customers. The clock read *10 p.m.* She should have been sound asleep by now but found it hard to focus on anything else except all the planning that was going to go towards the wedding cake.

She knew that this project was going to involve a lot of hard work, but she was determined to not let it phase her. She was going to pour her heart and soul into it, and nothing was going to stop her.

Chapter 2

The Long Way Home

Tuesday, May 28, 2019

Justin woke up a few hours later, awoken by someone nudging his shoulder. "Come on. Time to get up, sleepyhead," Charlotte whispered. He stretched out his arms, quickly blinking his eyes as they seemed to focus on her walking ahead of him to the airport's entrance. It slowly dawned on him that he had slept throughout the whole trip. "Oh, crap!" He quickly weaved in and out of the line of people, rushing to meet her at the luggage carousel.

Still a bit sleep deprived, he smiled when he caught a young woman looking through the luggage carousel. Her black hair was layered in neat rows of braids, complimenting her round face. The sun peeked through the airport's windows, showing the bronze glow of her skin. She wore a one-shoulder white top with a pair of navy blue jeans to complete the look.

"Charlotte!" he yelled out, hoping to catch her attention. She adjusted her focus from the carousel to him, waving back. He quickly ran towards her, encompassing her with a hug.

"Woah!" she said, trying to regain her balance. "Thanks!"

"How did you sleep?" he asked.

Charlotte shook her head. "Slept pretty well. I was trying to wake you up before the plane landed, but you were probably too tired to notice." She laughed until she noticed the dark circles under his eyes. Her eyebrows furrowed in concern. "Hey, you okay?"

Justin yawned in response, dragging his feet to where his luggage was. He looked through the carousel, his eyes landing on a dark green suitcase with a silver handle popping out from inside it. He lifted it up with a grunt, ignoring the sound of Charlotte's laughter from behind him. He turned towards her, a pinched expression on his face. "You could have helped me, you know?"

Charlotte laughed even louder. "It's not my fault that the bag weighs more than you. Besides, if I helped you carry your bag, it wouldn't have been as funny."

He struggled to maintain eye contact with her, her laughter turning into quiet snickers. He lifted his eyes to the sky, wondering why

God had decided to give him this kind of best friend.

"So how does it feel to be back in Atlanta?" Charlotte asked, looking at the time on her watch.

"It was a bit stressful, so it feels good to be home. I'm looking forward to seeing my friends again."

"Speaking of culinary school, Maddie's aunt let her take over her bakery business you guys used to work at as kids. I bet you're looking forward to seeing her again, huh, huh?" Charlotte asked, giving him a playful nudge.

With that one word, Justin's mind drifted to the one person that he would be happy to see again. He remembered the first time he met Maddie, at the start of high school eight years earlier.

* * *

It was a hot day in Atlanta on **Saturday, August 17, 2011** *as Justin wiped the sweat off his forehead, going into the air-conditioned coffee shop. His eyes flitted around the room as he noticed people chatting with one another while others were working on a paper that was probably due the following morning. Walking toward the couch, he failed to see someone was walking in the same direction. As the two bumped* into each other, the collision caused her to spill the latte onto her navy-blue jacket.

He scrambled to pick up the cup and return it to its owner. "Shit! I'm so sorry!" He looked up to see the person whom he had bumped into. He had to admit that the girl was rather good looking. Her curly, brown hair stopped at her shoulders, her glasses bringing attention to her brown eyes. Sunlight poured in from the windows, highlighting her light-brown skin.

He later admitted that Maddie was a bit awkward, but found himself infatuated with her from the start. There was a sort of endearing charm to her that he found himself drawn to, that reached beyond physical attraction, and for that reason, he wanted to get to know her more.

"No problem. I should have looked where I was going," she said.

She was about to walk away when Justin called out to her.

"Wait!"

Maddie turned around, waiting to hear his response. "Yeah?"

He gulped, taking a deep breath. "Can I at least buy you another drink? You know, since I caused you to drop it."

She bit her lip, turning her head to the side. After a moment, she nodded. "Sure, but it's only fair that I get to know the guy who's offering to buy my drink."

"Sounds like a deal." He walked over to the cashier to ask for another drink. He turned around, rubbing the back of his head. "Um, what was it you wanted again?"

She shook her head, amused as she stated the order to the cashier, who proceeded to ring it up.

A few minutes later, the two walked over to the couch, with Maddie getting out her sketchpad.

"Whatcha drawing?" he asked, peering over her shoulder to get a good look.

With a hesitant glance, she held up the drawing she had been working on. The girl was dressed in what looked a 90s costume, swaying her hips to the beat of the music.

He looked up at her. "That's really good. You should show draw more often. With a bit of hard work, you could make your drawings into something worth selling."

Maddie hid her face from his view, looking down with a smile. "Thanks!" She tucked a strand of hair behind her ear. "This is actually my first one." She had been about to draw the girl's glasses when she looked up. "What about you? What hobbies do you have?"

Justin turned his head to the side. "Do you count listening to musical soundtracks as a hobby?"

She giggled, nodding her head. "I guess. Do you have any others?"

He tugged at his shirt. The only other hobby he had was baking.

I, um, I like to bake sweets," he muttered, turning his attention to the people around him. He blinked, trying to seem like he didn't care what she thought, but that couldn't be further from the truth. He finally decided to look up at her, and was surprised to see that her eyes had lit up in a way he had never seen before.

"I've never met a guy who's liked to bake before. That's really cool!" she said, suppressing a laugh at the way his eyes widened. She gave him a lopsided grin. "What? Did you think I would have judged you? Sorry to break it to you, Skyscraper, but I'm not the type of person to judge people on their hobbies."

* * *

Charlotte waved a hand in front of him, tapping her foot. "*Hello?* Earth to Justin?"

He snapped out of his thoughts as Charlotte's words brought him back to reality. "Sorry, what did you say? I must have zoned out for a second."

17

She shook her head. "Man, you must have it bad for her!"

Justin shoved her shoulder, hard. "I do not!"

She resisted the urge to roll her eyes. "Sure you don't. Just don't expect her to come *running* into your arms. You rejected her in 11th grade, remember?"

"I let her down *gently*," he emphasized, his muscles becoming tense. He should have known that his decision to tell Charlotte about that would come to bite him in the ass.

"Nicely, harshly, it doesn't matter!" Charlotte hissed. "Rejection *hurts*, Justin. No matter how much you try to convince yourself that it doesn't." She marched toward the entrance of the airport, waiting for him to catch up with her.

Justin sighed, a cloud hanging over his head as his anticipated reunion with Maddie began to leave a bitter taste in his mouth. The only reason he rejected Maddie was because he wasn't sure about his feelings for her and didn't want to lead her on. Plus, she already had her hands full between juggling her job of running her bakery part-time and college classes. He wasn't sure if the two of them could handle a relationship at the time.

He shook his head. They had been best friends since high school, for crying out loud!

He remembered when she had told him a part of her past, specifically why she transferred to Lakeview High. Justin knew Maddie had been bullied, but he wasn't sure to what extent because he didn't want to pry, for fear of making her uncomfortable. He just hoped that his rejection wouldn't cause them to drift apart.

"Hey, wait a minute. Why are you so protective over Maddie, anyway?" he asked, once he caught up with Charlotte.

Charlotte turned around, a soft smile on her face. "She's my best friend. I'm always gonna be protective over her. She's really sweet and deserves the best that life has to offer. I admire that she stands up for herself when she needs to."

He chuckled. "Don't I know it. There was one time that in high school, I tried to make her laugh with a pun, and she punched my arm."

She snorted. "We all remember your *pitiful* attempt at flirting with her."

Justin got his phone from his pocket to book Uber to get to his house. "It wasn't *that* bad," he muttered, waiting for the car to come to pick them up.

As the vehicle arrived at its destination, they checked for the license plate number, making sure that it was the right car.

"Hello, are you Terrence by any chance?" Justin asked, while Charlotte made sure to share their Uber ride with both her parents as well as his.

The man tipped his cap off to them. "Yes, Sir."

When the two realized that this Uber driver was the right one, they hopped into the backseat, eager to get home after a long flight. Justin was on the left side while Charlotte was on the right, texting her family and friends that they'd be back soon.

The driver spoke up. "So, where are you guys headed to?"

"Covington, sir," Charlotte replied, speaking for the two of them before Justin could get a word in edgewise. The driver of the vehicle looked back at her through the rearview mirror, smiling. "I live there myself. Beautiful city. Not too crowded either."

Justin nodded in agreement. "Yeah, we just got back from Indianapolis. Went there for culinary school. It was fun, but it's good to be home."

Charlotte snickered, turning to face Justin. "Dude, please." She averted her gaze to the driver. "He's only saying that because he gets to see the girl he's had a crush on for five years."

The driver chuckled, causing Justin to avoid his gaze and look out the window. Maddie was just a friend, right? So why did it feel like she was more than that?

Chapter 3

No Ordinary Day

Wednesday, May 29, 2019

The warmth of the sunlight on her skin alongside the cool breeze made for a perfect day. Business was slow but steady as usual. It had some orders coming in, but only every once in a while. It needed something to get people talking about it to the point where it would be well known across town.

Maddie took a moment to step outside the shop as she reveled in the joy of seeing the words *Creative Confections* written in big, shiny letters on the storefront, the golden glow of the sun reflecting off of them. Catching her reflection on the front window, she scrunched her face in disgust. She was covered in flour from head to toe while her hair looked like a bird's nest. Dressed in a casual black top with blue jeans, she wore a black apron with white stencils of various flowers on every inch of it, with her hair wrapped up in a neat bun.

As she entered the shop, jazz music could be heard playing from the speakers as she went around the coffee tables. They were a rich brown with a glass center underneath their legs. She looked to her left to see the bags she and her mom had decorated for the big round loaves of fresh bread that they made together. Their aroma filled the shop with a slightly sweet, comforting smell. *Speaking of smells...* Cinnamon. She needed cinnamon if she was going to make her world-famous cinnamon cake. Her reputation counted on this cake, and, as she scoured the shelves for the vital spice, continued to remind herself that she couldn't afford to screw this up. At that moment, she remembered that she put the spice in a different area rather than where it was supposed to be.

"You idiot!" Maddie hissed at herself, looking in every corner of the kitchen. "Where is it? Where is it?!" she repeated with increasing frustration, her voice sounding more frenzied by the minute.

Ring! The door sounded as someone entered the shop. Looking up from her search, she smiled when her friend Amber walked towards her with a spring in her step, her wavy, blonde hair swishing in the breeze. It was clear that she had been in the sun, her fair skin turning a pale pink as a result of being in its rays. Her blue eyes lit up in excitement. "Hey Maddie! Are we still on for hanging out at the mall today?" she asked.

"You're here! Can you please help me out?" Maddie pleaded.

Amber frowned, shooting Maddie a tense smile. "Please tell me you didn't forget."

Maddie tore her gaze away from her. Her brown eyes spared her an apologetic glance. "Sorry... I had a last-minute order, and you know how things are with the business right now." She blew a strand of her hair out of her eyes. "I'm looking for cinnamon. I need it for a recipe."

A look of understanding came across Amber's face, noticing the bags under her friend's eyes. "Don't worry. I'm here to help." She gave her a salute before rushing off to the kitchen cabinets and rummaging through them until she found the cinnamon she was looking for.

Maddie let out a satisfied sigh. "Thanks, you're a lifesaver."

Amber tried to contain her laughter when she took in her friend's disheveled appearance.

Maddie raised an eyebrow, unimpressed. "Laugh all you want, but I bet you won't be laughing once you taste the cake." She fumbled with the flour and cinnamon as she put it into the butter and sugar mixture.

"You sure you don't need any help?" Amber called out with a grimace as Maddie scurried around the kitchen.

After Maddie wiped the sweat off her forehead, she washed her hands for what she thought was the tenth time that day. "I'm good, just about to put the cake in the oven," she shouted over her shoulder, buttering the cake pans.

"Just watching you run back and forth in the kitchen looks exhausting. Let's play something different!" Amber suggested. She walked toward Maddie's laptop to stop the jazz music playing softly through the speakers before tapping her phone as she searched for the Spotify app to play *Me and My Girls* by Fifth Harmony.

"Oh no, not this again," Maddie whined, watching as Amber grabbed a wooden spoon from the utensil holder and sang into it like a microphone. Amber continued to sing the first few lines with confidence, twirling around like she had no care in the world.

When it came down to the second part, she looked at Maddie, waiting for her to play along. Amber knew Maddie didn't like singing in public. What if someone heard her? She kept herself occupied by wiping down the kitchen table, carrying the bags full of jars of baking ingredients to the cabinet where she kept them. Dusting off her hands, her eyes darted to the window, making sure no one could see her and then, with a deep breath, opened her mouth to sing.

Maddie started out in almost a whisper, singing in a timid voice. As the song continued to play, her voice became louder and bolder, her confidence growing. When she finished, Amber clapped. "See? You're already getting out of your comfort zone. I'm so proud of you."

Maddie pinched her nose, hoping that no one heard her awful singing voice while Amber felt a sense of pride wash over her as she watched the brunette come out of her shell. She was then pulled into a hug.

"Thanks, Amber. But this is the last time you're gonna hear me sing, okay?"

Amber frowned. "Fine, but just because *Justin* heard you sing–"

"Please don't bring that up," Maddie said, bringing the cake from out of the oven and putting it on a cooling rack.

The blonde winced. "Sorry... I forgot you tend to get easily embarrassed."

"It's okay." The brunette fidgeted with the purity ring on her finger and let out a nervous chuckle. "Speaking of Justin, I still remember the day we first met."

Maddie's thoughts took her back to eight years ago. Justin was sweet as he could be, carrying most of the conversation to get to know her more, even after she acted like a total klutz when they quite literally ran into each other. She remembered how he laughed at how awkward she was, yet felt like he was the kind of friend you could talk to for hours on end.

Amber sighed. "I wish you'd sing more often. I love how carefree you seem to be when you sing," she admitted, noticing her friend roll her eyes. She walked towards the fridge to grab an apple to eat and looked up from the array of items she gathered, slowly grabbing the bundle of green ribbon and scissors from her hands.

Walking towards the kitchen table, Maddie laid the things down in a neat row. She smiled as the two of them packaged the cake in bags to get the customer's order ready.

Amber looked at her expectantly. "By the way, you never told me the story of how you acquired the bakery in the first place."

Maddie laughed, knowing Amber was a big fan of stories. "Fine, I'll tell you. Just don't make a big deal out of it, okay?" She ran to get her bag that was sitting on the chair a few feet away. "Thanks for helping me out. I don't know how I would have managed without you." she continued, finding what she was looking for and handing it to Amber.

She nodded, grabbing a chair from the dining table to sit on. She peered inside the envelope to see a twenty dollar bill. "Oh no, Maddie, I couldn't." she argued, handing the envelope back to the brunette.

"Please? It's the least I could do after you helped me out today. I won't take no for an answer, Missy!" Maddie scolded, giving her friend an expression that held no room for argument.

Amber rolled her eyes. "Okay, well, thank you!" she said, looking up at her in gratitude. "Now tell me the story of how you and your aunt made a deal. I'm so bored!" She grabbed a chair from the dining table to sit on.

Maddie put her hands in her laptop, trying to remember how the conversation went. "My aunt wanted to close the place down because she didn't have any need for it anymore after her fashion business took off, so I convinced her to give the place to me, provided that I make good use of it."

The expression on Amber's face was full of curiosity. "So how did you convince her that you were the right person to continue with the bakery then?"

The brunette looked out the window as the memories started to resurface again. "I remember the times I used to help her in the kitchen," she continued. "Mmm, I can almost smell her freshly baked chocolate chip cookies. Customers came in and out, smiling each time they bought a freshly baked treat. Every morning after I finished my classes in high school, working at the bakery was my part-time job. It was one of the things that made my relationship with my aunt stronger," she finished.

"Aw, that's so cute!" Amber gushed.

Maddie stayed silent, averting her eyes from her to one of the pre-packaged cakes. She loved working for her aunt during that time she started high school. It gave her some time to relax after classes were done for the day. Things got even more interesting when she met Justin. Maddie was surprised he had taken her up on the offer to stop by where she worked a few weeks after they had met. She had never seen anyone so excited to come to see her before, and for him to keep coming to see her... well, that was just an added bonus. Maddie just hoped that Amber wouldn't remember that little detail.

"Hang on. Didn't Justin use to be a regular customer at your aunt's bakery?"

"Yeah..." Maddie stayed silent. "I decided to confess my feelings to him and... well... He didn't accept them," she said, the hurtful reminder of rejection creeping into her mind.

Amber handed her a tissue from the box of tissues lying on the table beside them. "Aw, honey... "

Maddie took the tissue from Amber's hand. "It's okay. I've accepted the fact that Justin may never reciprocate my feelings. I mean, the reason I fell for him in the first place was because he was a sweet and sincere person." *He still is.* She remembered the last time they video chatted with one another, the smile on his face when she told him about her cat.

Amber tapped her chin. "Maybe those two years of culinary school did him good. Things change, you know."

Not that quickly, Maddie mused, as she continued to package the desserts with Amber while reminiscing about her first meeting with the boy who stole her heart. She felt her blood pressure begin to rise as a single tear trailed down her cheek. Clenching her fists, she shook her head. *She had to put her mind on the task at hand. She couldn't afford to have any distractions or make any mistakes.* The whirlwind of emotions coursing through her veins caused her to take a sharp intake of breath. She couldn't afford to lose focus. Not now. Not ever.

Chapter 4

When I See You Again

Thursday, May 30, 2019

Maddie slowly trudged into the university's library, her feet stopping near the security entrance. She tried not to think about how her day had gone so far. She had been unprepared for today's sociology reflection paper and, as a result, bombed it or at least that's what it seemed like anyway. Time had seemed to slow down for her at that moment, trying to focus on how much time she had until the professor collected the papers. She couldn't let that happen again. She needed this class to graduate. At least her professor dropped the lowest quiz grade, she was thankful for that.

Walking past the library's reception desk, her gaze turned towards a guy with vibrant brown skin wearing a navy blue polo shirt with light blue jeans. Maddie recognized him as one of her closest friends, Brian. She smiled when he spared her a wave as she walked up to him. She didn't know when they had met, but from the few times they talked to each other, he seemed like a pretty cool guy.

"Hey, Maddie. What's up?" Brian said, looking up from something he was working on.

Maddie sighed. "Nothing much. I just got this order from my friend's aunt. She wants me to make a cake for her."

Brian nodded. "Cool."

She beamed. "Yeah, I'm pretty excited about it. She's supposed to call me in the next few minutes or so."

He laughed. "Well, don't let me keep you. Good luck!"

Instead of heading deeper into the library, Maddie walked into the cafe. As soon as she plopped down on one of the cafe's couches, her phone rang. *She just couldn't catch a break, now could she?* Almost immediately, she shuffled her fingers through her book bag, trying to find it. At last, she felt her hands touch the item and pressed the answer button. "Hello?"

"Hello, Maddie. It's good to hear from you again. Your mom gave me your number, and I just wanted to let you know the details regarding the cake I ordered."

She smiled, recognizing Miss Caroline's voice. It was what you could expect from an influential person such as herself. Her voice sounded friendly, but held a bit of professionalism. Her heart started thumping inside her chest, not from fear but from the excitement rising within her. She unzipped her book bag to get her notebook and a pencil to jot down the details. "I'm ready. What would you want the cake to look like?" she asked, feeling the adrenaline course through her veins.

"I'd like a five-tier rich, decadent chocolate truffle cake with New Years' Eve sparklers on top of it and fake cranberry plants around the bottom of the cake. The cake mustn't be too sweet nor too bitter. They must have fancy chocolate buttercream flowers all around the top of the cake, but not too much that it overcrowds where the sparklers are."

Thoughts whizzed around Maddie's mind. *She said truffle, right? She hadn't made truffle filling before, but that didn't mean she couldn't learn.* Maddie chuckled a little louder than usual, attracting the attention of the customers nearby, who looked around in concern as to where that god-awful noise came from. "Okay, is that all?" Maddie asked, wiping sweat off her forehead.

"That's it, sweetie! Thank you so much for doing this. You don't know how many bakeries I've thought of calling these past few months, only to find out that I'd need a two months' notice. I was just about ready to give up, but then your mom recommended you, and oh, I'm about to cry."

Maddie could sense Miss Caroline dabbing her eyes with a tissue right about now. She rolled her eyes at her semantics. *Does she have to be such a drama queen, though?*

"What was that, dear?" Miss Caroline asked.

Maddie panicked, dropping the phone, and picking it up from the floor. "Oh, nothing, Miss Caroline." She cleared her throat, taking a sip from the bottle of water she had beside her. "I'll make sure that the cake exceeds your expectations.

She could picture Miss Caroline grinning from ear to ear at her response. "Oh, I'm so happy to hear that, dear. Have a good day."

"You too." Maddie hung up the phone, laying back on the couch to relax. She felt someone tap her on the shoulder and whipped her head around. "What?" she snapped. *So much for peace and quiet.*

The stranger put his hands up in defense. "Woah, sorry! Didn't know you were having one of *those* days... "

She blinked, recognizing the voice. "Justin."

An awkward silence passed between them, with Maddie's thoughts racing a mile a minute. She wondered if he felt as awkward as she did right now. She turned to look at him. He looked a little bit older now, but she could still recognize the same guy she had been best friends with for years. When they were younger, he looked a bit more bald. Whenever she asked about it, he always said his barber had given him a bad haircut and was waiting for his hair to grow back.

It seemed to her that ever since time passed, he had grown more mature than she had realized. His eyes looked a bit brighter than usual. *Well, as bright as someone with dark brown eyes could be anyway.* His hair had grown out a bit more and his voice had become a bit deeper since she last saw him. She couldn't help but admire the features that he had, as well as his lovable personality.

Justin looked back at her, tilting his head to the side. "Yeah, it's me. I haven't seen you in forever. How have things been?" he asked, walking around the couch to sit beside her.

Maddie got up to give him a hug. "Honestly? It's been a bit stressful since I've decided to go back to college to get my bachelor's degree in English, but it's going well. Secondly, what do you mean by *those* days?" she repeated, putting air quotes around the word "those."

Justin wrinkled his nose. "I meant that anything that can go wrong will go wrong." He raised an eyebrow. "What did you think I meant?"

She cleared her throat. "Um, never mind." Proceeding to put her hands on her knees, she found herself rocking back and forth. *Justin's here. He's really here... in this building.*

Her eyes flitted around the room, amazed at how the barista managed to make the coffee smell so good. Maddie had a new appreciation for her, despite all the orders she had to fulfill. She got up and decided to get a coffee to keep her mind off the awkwardness. "Hello, can I please have a butterscotch latte?"

The barista looked up at Maddie, holding her gaze with her tired eyes. "Of course, that would be–" She yawned. "Excuse me, I stayed up late to study for a test last night."

Maddie nodded in understanding, admiring how the young girl juggled both college classes and work. After ordering and receiving her drink a few minutes later, Maddie went back to where Justin was and sat down beside him.

He opened his mouth to say something, then closed it.

Maddie turned her body towards him, making eye contact. "Okay, I'm going to be real with you here. I hate awkward silence."

He laughed. "Same here. So, how has college life and the bakery been going?"

She let out a sigh. "They've both been... going. I mean, I've been getting good grades, but with the reading and picking up side gigs for editing work, it's been challenging at times to juggle both. Good thing the job was short term, or else I wouldn't have gotten an A in my English and History classes."

"I can relate to that. I remember you telling me you tried juggling a job with your summer classes one time and that it didn't go well. I'm happy to hear you've learned from that experience."

"Yep... " Maddie could feel the awkward silence hanging in the air again. She fiddled with the notebook in her hands, desperate for anything to break the silence. Justin pursued his lips while she avoided eye contact. "So how did everything at Silver Oaks go for you? Was it everything you hoped and dreamed it would be?" she asked. *This guy was her best friend. Surely she could talk to him without getting nervous, right?*

He fidgeted with his hands. "Well, it wasn't the best, but it wasn't the worst, either."

She looked at her friend like he had grown a second head. "How come? I thought it was supposed to be fun."

He closed his eyes, thinking back to his time in culinary school. "Well, it had its moments. First day of culinary school, people expect you to pick up the pace in the kitchen and toughen up whenever you get a scratch or something," he continued. "I remember the first few days. I accidentally cut myself with a sharp knife and had to get bandages for it, although I probably should have asked someone to keep an eye on the stew I was cooking since I put it on high heat."

Maddie rubbed his shoulder, seeing him wince at the memory. "When I remembered I had put something on the stove, I quickly rushed back to it, but it was too late. The stew had already been burnt to a crisp. Even the bottom of the pot was black. When the head chef came to see what happened, I was afraid he was going to rip me a new one. Unfortunately, what he did was even worse. He made an example out of me, telling his students that I was a primary example of what *not* to do. Even though we had a good chuckle out of it, I was still a little embarrassed."

Justin shook his head, a haunted look in his eyes. "After that happened, the students and the head chef left me one by one, except for Charlotte, who stayed behind to teach me how to cook the soup properly and move on to more challenging dishes. Charlotte works in our college library, so remind me to show you the department where she works sometime."

He reached down into his book bag to get his textbook. "We worked throughout the night, with her directing me and me following her orders. We made a pretty good team back then. Maybe even more than good."

She clenched her fists. Justin and Charlotte had started dating, and he had the nerve not to even tell her? "Sorry to hear that happened, but I'm glad you had your girlfriend to support you-"

"Girlfriend?" Justin threw his head back, laughing. "You've got it all wrong, Maddie. Sure, she was a good support system to help me get through culinary school, but we didn't end up getting together if that's what you're thinking."

She turned away from Justin, feeling a blush creep up toward her cheeks. "Oh, I'm sorry. I didn't mean to assume–" She groaned, wondering how she came to that conclusion. *Way to go, idiot.*

He waved his hand. "Don't worry. Charlotte's not my type. Anyway, I realized that even though I have a degree in pastry arts, I needed something more solid. So, a few months before I finished culinary school, I decided to apply to Lakeview so that I could finish my degree in Rhetoric and Composition. I got an email back, saying that I had been accepted, so I decided to register for classes as soon as possible."

Maddie tackled him with a hug. "That's amazing, Justin. I'm so proud of you."

"Thanks, Cupcake. Oh!" He snapped his fingers. "By the way, you haven't answered my original question."

She shuffled in her seat, her eyes going wide. She found herself fumbling over her words. "W-what about?"

Justin gave her a pointed look. "Don't play dumb with me, Mads. You know *exactly* what I'm talking about. You just tried to avoid answering when I asked you how the bakery was going." He continued. "Go on, out with it–if you want to, that is. I don't want to make you feel uncomfortable."

She let out a laugh that seemed forced. "It's been okay, I guess."

Justin raised an eyebrow. "Just okay?"

Maddie turned her head to the side, taking a deep breath. She clenched her fists. *He's not obligated to know what happened.* "It's none of your business," she snapped, causing Justin to frown.

The two stood side by side, unable to look each other in the eyes.

After what seemed like forever to her, Maddie spoke up. "I'm sorry. I didn't mean to snap at you like that." She turned her head to the side. "I'll tell you what's up, but only if you *promise* not to tell anyone."

He motioned to his lips, zipping them, and throwing away the key. Maddie wondered how he always managed to switch from being so serious to playful in the blink of an eye.

She took a deep breath and began telling Justin about the order his aunt had given to her, how she didn't know the first thing about making truffle filling but that she was willing to learn if he could teach her. Maddie looked into his eyes, accepting full responsibility for her actions. *She shouldn't be upset just because she was worried about what Justin would think. He was never the type to judge people anyway.* She opened her eyes and was surprised to find his hand lying on top of hers.

"Maddie... " Justin began. "I understand that you have a good heart, but you can't always help everyone."

Maddie let out a light chuckle. "I know... "

"But... " he continued. "I am proud of you and the way you jumped at the chance to help my aunt. You don't understand how much I admire you for taking on a project so big. May I make a suggestion, though?"

She looked up to see he had moved his hand from her hand to her shoulder.

"How about you let me help you? I learned to make truffle filling back in culinary school, so I could give you some pointers. That way, we can finish the job together, and you won't have to go back to my aunt, empty-handed. You still have classes on Tuesdays and Thursdays, right?"

Maddie nodded.

"Cool! My classes fall under those days too. So, here's what we'll do: we'll work on baking simple little things, then move on to harder things on Wednesdays and Fridays."

Maddie thought about his offer for a second. "Can I do something for you in return?"

Justin blinked. "I'm not looking to get something out of this, Mads. I'm doing it to help you grow your confidence."

She bit her lip. "But it doesn't seem very fair that you help me and get nothing in return." She turned her head, trying to think of something he could need help with.

Justin sighed. "How about this? You can help me with my English homework. I heard from Brian that you're really good. So... do we have ourselves a deal?" He brought out his hand for her to shake.

"Deal!" She shook his hand, her mind racing with the thought of working together with her crush of four years. *Wait, no, he wasn't her crush. Just a friend.* She had already been down that rabbit hole and wasn't sure she didn't want to go down that path again.

Chapter 5

Practice Makes Perfect

Friday, May 31, 2019

Justin sat on his living room couch, watching Maddie throw a handful of popcorn into her mouth. He sighed, willing himself to get up from the couch. "Come on, Maddie. Let's get started."

He heard Maddie groan as she followed him to the front door, shaking her head. "No, no, no. I don't think that's such a good idea," she said, rubbing her arm.

"Come on, Maddie! We've been going through easy recipes for about two weeks now, and I think it's time to go through some practice runs on how to make this sort of thing."

Maddie bit her lip. "I don't know. What if I mess up?"

Justin knelt down to her level. "I know you can do this, Firecracker. Your sister believes in you, your mom believes in you, and most importantly, I believe in you. I know you have some trouble understanding instructions, but just know that I'll be patient with you. We'll get through them together, okay."

She took a deep breath. "Okay, I'm ready."

He grinned at her. "That's the spirit! Now, let's get started." The two got in the car as soon as he closed the front door behind them. Before she knew it, they were in front of the bakery. When they walked inside, the first thing she noticed was the array of ingredients they needed to make truffle laid out for them to see. "I see you were already prepared, huh?"

"A chef is always ready for a good challenge," he said with pride.

She suppressed a laugh, sputtering like an old water faucet.

"Lucky for you, I already bought the kind of chocolate we need. It's called couverture chocolate," Justin said, getting a washed pot from the bakery cabinet. "It's a bar of very high-quality chocolate that contains more cocoa butter than you would normally find in the baking chocolate you buy from Walmart," he continued.

He got under the table to grab a clean pot from the cabinet, putting it on the stove. "Okay, so the first thing you want to do is put on the stove. Now answer this: how hot does the stove need to be to make truffle filling?" he questioned.

"Hmmm, medium to high height, I guess?" she answered.

"Let's try it out and see for ourselves," he replied back.

Justin watched as Maddie turned the knob to where it said six while he poured a little bit of chocolate into the double boiler, grabbing a wooden spoon from the drawer and stirring the chocolate. "I forgot how much fun baking could be–oh, is that a blue jay?" she commented, rushing to the window to take a peek at blue-feathered beauty.

She let out an "aw" when the bird flew into the trees, causing Justin to suppress a chuckle at her enthusiasm. After putting the pot on the stove, he added the chocolate in while Maddie turned the knob to low heat and slowly poured the heavy cream into the pot. She mixed the chocolate and cream together until the delicious concoction looked silky.

"Now add two teaspoons of orange zest to it and taste it," he instructed.

Maddie did as he instructed, tasting the chocolate before and after she added the orange zest in.

"Do you taste any difference?" he asked, hoping she would.

"Yeah, it complements the flavor of the chocolate."

He nodded. "It's all about experimenting and finding out which flavors work best with one another. Good thing we only made a small batch."

She turned her head to the side. "So, what do we do now?"

He looked lost for words as he tried to think of something. "We could put the chocolate in an ice cube tray, freeze it and then eat it."

"Sounds good to me," Maddie said.

* * *

An hour later, the two got in the car, driving back to Maddie's house.

Opening the front door, she zoomed past him to sit on the couch.

He raised an eyebrow. "Where do you get all that energy from?"

She shrugged. "You may never know."

Turning on the TV, the two watched Yumeiro Pâtissiers together, enjoying each other's company.

Justin turned to Maddie. "I remember the first time you introduced me to this anime. When was that, two years ago?"

Maddie sat there, her eyes glued to the decadent desserts. She never knew how much better it looked in the anime. "Yeah, you decided that we should have a movie day after you saw how upset I was over my math test."

Justin snorted. "I didn't blame you one bit

for feeling that way. The professor was nice, and all, but the concepts he taught were difficult at times," he confessed.

"I remember asking the professor a whole bunch of questions about the concept, trying to figure out what a parabola is and how to put it into my calculator." Maddie bit her lip. "The class was probably annoyed with me, though."

Justin turned away from her, fighting back a blush.

"You okay?" she asked, noticing how Justin had turned away from her.

His voice cracked. "Yeah, I'm fine," he replied, clearing his throat. Staring at the TV, he thought of the day he showed up at her house with snickerdoodle cookies and spent time with her. He turned his gaze towards Maddie, watching as a grin appeared on her face.

Five years ago, on Valentine's Day, Maddie had confided to him that she was sad that she didn't get a present that day, so she was surprised to see him on her doorstep with a bag of her favorite cookies and an anime to watch. He had basked in the comfortable silence as he thought back to that day.

Justin remembered how a smile made its way onto her face as she took a bite out of one of the cookies. He loved making people happy, regardless of whether they thanked him for it or not.

"Sorry, I've been quiet all this time," he said, bringing her thoughts back to the present. "It's just that... the way you bit your lip just now... It was cute... adorable, actually."

Maddie was taken aback by his response. "Oh... Well, thanks."

Justin turned his attention back to the TV. "W-we should probably get back to watching the anime, though."

Her cheeks looked flushed as she turned towards him to ask a question. "Do I have *that* much of an effect on you, Justin?"

He turned towards her, looking at her with confidence. "You most definitely do, Cupcake." He gingerly brushed his hand against hers, waiting for a reaction.

Maddie inched closer towards him, taking one deep breath after the other.

Justin paused the show for a minute. "Maddie, breathe. It's okay. You're safe, alright? I'm sorry if what I did made you uncomfortable." He could hear her breathing begin to return to its normal rate. "I can stop if you want me to?"

Maddie turned her face towards him. "What if..." She took another deep breath.

"The thought of your hand on top of mine makes me happy yet nervous?"

Justin tried to gauge her reaction. Her brown eyes showed their usual sparkle, but something felt different. They held a bit of uncertainty, afraid of getting hurt, afraid of being vulnerable.

He opened his mouth to speak. "I know I hurt your feelings in the past, Cupcake, and I'm sorry. But if I had stringed you along when I wasn't even sure of how I felt, would that have been any better?"

Maddie mulled over his answer, then shook her head. "I think I would have been even more upset, if that's possible." She rested her chin in the palm of her hands. "I'm older now though, so I understand why you made that decision."

Justin looked at her for a second, as the sunlight poured in through the window. The sun was shining down on her, showing how graceful she looked. *Even when doing something so simple, she still had the ability to look adorable.*

She turned her attention from the show to him as he turned his head away, letting out an innocent whistle. She chuckled. "Silly Skyscraper."

He felt his heart skip a beat. Why did being called Skyscraper cause a smile to

come to his face? "Sly firecracker."
She inched her face closer. "You know you love me."
Justin gulped, putting his finger on her nose to slightly push her away. "That's for me to know and you to try to figure out." He could feel it. *This girl was going to be the death of him, sooner rather than later.*

Chapter 6

Infinite Possibilities

Wednesday, June 5, 2019

Maddie was with Justin in her home's kitchen, looking at a video of her favorite YouTuber making her famous carrot cake cupcakes. "Okay, so we need flour, butter, sugar, eggs... " She looked at the list of ingredients her idol put in the description of her video. She bit her lip, trying to figure out the best way to go about this. She felt his presence as he walked up toward her, looking at the recipe along with her.

"Find anything?"

She turned around, finding herself nose to nose with Justin. *Too close. Too close!*

"Excuse me," Maddie said, moving a step backward.

"Sorry!" Justin exclaimed, turning his face away from her.

She felt her face heat up. *Why did he have to look so cute? Why?* She turned her attention back to the video, getting her eyes to focus on what the woman was saying. She turned her eyes to him to find him looking at her again. "What is it?"

Justin shifted his body around. "Just out of curiosity, have you ever tried to just, you know, not bake without a recipe?"

Maddie looked disgusted, crossing her arms. "No, but it's better that way. Then I won't make a mistake. The first time I tried a carrot cake recipe out, it didn't turn out that well."

He raised an eyebrow. "What happened?"

She turned away from his gaze, letting out a huff. "It's embarrassing," she whined.

He chuckled. "I won't make fun of you, scout's honor."

Turning to look at him, Maddie noticed the curious expression on his face. "Okay. Well, I was mixing the ingredients for the recipe, then my cat, Clara, came in, so I momentarily got distracted with playing with her for a bit. After playing with her, I washed my hands and continued to add the rest of the ingredients. When it was done, I gave a piece to my dad to taste."

She groaned, remembering the next part. "My dad's face had scrunched up when he tasted it, so I had a taste as well. It was salty."

She heard Justin snort, trying to conceal his laughter. "You promised you wouldn't laugh!" she said, giving him a pout.

After a few seconds, he stopped laughing long enough to notice the look on her face.

"I'm sorry, Mads. I'm not laughing at you, I swear." It took him a moment for his laughter to turn into quiet chuckles. "Don't be embarrassed. You just got a bad recipe, that's all. Whether or not it was because of your cat, I don't know."

He scratched the corner of his mouth. "Regardless of the experience, you have to learn to trust yourself when it comes to experimenting with recipes."

Justin walked over to where his school bag was, grabbing his phone from inside and tapping at the screen. "There's this recipe that I've made countless times. We could make that instead of carrot cake, and I could walk you through it if you'd like. Just remember my advice, okay?"

Maddie nodded, happy that he was supporting her in what she needed. She peeked at his phone, noticing the word "castella" written at the top of the note. "What's that?"

"It's a type of Japanese sponge cake that I think you might like making since you love Japanese desserts and the language, of course," Justin explained.

Her eyes softened, a look of gratitude reflected in her eyes. "You remembered."

He whipped his head in her direction. "Why would I forget such an important detail about you? It's what makes you unique."

Maddie smiled.

"And I'm your number one friend in the world," he bragged.

She laughed. "True." She looked at the ingredients laid out on the table and put the carrots and butter back in the fridge. She felt Justin's gaze linger on her as she swapped some of the ingredients out for new ones: all-purpose flour for bread, white sugar for demerara sugar, and honey out from inside the cabinet. She went to work, putting the milk and honey in a separate, heatproof bowl, whisking the ingredients with speed. "Can you put this in the microwave for me, please?"

Justin grabbed the bowl from her, putting it in the microwave for about ten seconds, then taking the container out and putting it back onto the table, standing by her side.

She used the hand mixer that was sitting near the sugar, beating the eggs at medium speed. She poured in the sugar, stopping when she found no more granules of the sweet substance while Justin sifted the bread flour, as the particles started to fill up the large bowl.

She added half of the milk and honey mixture, swapping between it and the bread flour, interchanging one for the other. Adding a teaspoon of baking powder to the mix, Maddie poured the batter into the square cake pan, which was lined up with parchment paper.

Justin took the pan from her, putting it in the preheated oven. He gave Maddie a high five. "You did it, Maddie. Now we wait."

Maddie looked at him, realizing she knew nothing about where he grew up. "I just realized something. You know where I grew up, but I don't know a thing about your childhood."

He chuckled. "Okay, pull up a chair and I'll tell you."

She did as was told, sitting down at the table. Resting her chin in the palm of her hands, her eyes flickered with excitement.

He took up a seat beside her. "Well, first thing you should know is that I grew up in Madrid." He had a faraway look in his eyes. "My parents were bilingual, so I ended up speaking a mixture of Spanish and English for most of my life."

Maddie noticed the way his eyes twinkled when he talked about his hometown. She was touched that he shared this part of him with her.

Justin turned to look at her. "If you end up going there, it's important to learn the language. It will make speaking to people a whole lot easier. Plus, learning a new language is always fun." He gave her a lopsided grin. "I could try teaching you if you want."

Her eyes lit up with longing. "Could you? I would really appreciate that. I took a few Spanish classes during my summer and fall semesters at Lakeview University, but I couldn't immerse myself into the language for some reason."

Justin laughed. "Probably because you were doing it for homework. When you're learning a language because you *want* to, it's much more fun. Believe me." He stayed silent for a moment. "We had lived in a modest, two-story house. We often ate together in the dining area, having causal conversations with each other. In Madrid, you usually have two breakfast meals: a small, light meal before having a bigger meal midmorning."

"Sounds like my kind of place," Maddie said, before trying to think of another question to ask him. "What did your house look like?"

Justin chewed his lip. "We lived in a modest house. Two stories high, that sort of thing. I had my own room while my parents lived in the main one. Our house was decorated with pictures from when I was about one year old to the time I turned sixteen. There are pictures of me and mi familia making funny faces and some of my cousins as well."

Maddie drummed her fingers on the table. "Do you visit often?"

He smiled, happy that someone was taking an interest in learning more about him. "Every couple of years, yeah. I've found that while some things remain the same, a lot has changed since I've been there. People often take what's known as *siestas* there, but there are more people speaking English, better ways of getting where you want to go and more options for eating out."

Maddie looked up at him, hearing a sigh escape from his lips. "Do you miss being home?"

Justin laughed quietly. "More than I care to admit, Cupcake." He cupped her cheek, trailing his finger down the side of her face. "But if I didn't move to Atlanta, I wouldn't have had a chance to meet you, mi reina." He removed his hand from her cheek, loving the fact that he had gotten her flustered for a moment.

Her face burned crimson under his gaze. "Pretty sure that was a compliment, but I have yet to know what that means."

He chuckled. "Don't worry, I'll teach you the language one of these days."

A few minutes later, the cake was done and ready to be eaten. Justin cut up the cake with a pie slicer. "Go on, you deserve to have the first taste."

Maddie gulped, her confidence wavering. *Well, at least she tried her best, right?* She closed her eyes, taking a bite out of the dessert and was pleasantly surprised at its sweet flavor. "It's soft and spongy, but it doesn't taste too sweet," she thought aloud.

Her gaze turned to Justin, who looked like a parent who was proud of his or her child. "I'm so proud of you, Maddie. You did it."

Maddie's cheeks flushed at the praise, realizing that all she needed was a push in the right direction. "Think we could get started on me helping you with your English homework?"

"Aw, but I hate doing homework," he whined.

Maddie put a hand on his shoulder. "It's not my favorite thing in the world either, but we have to get it done at some point. Otherwise, it's just going to pile up." She walked towards the living room, with him trailing close behind. Taking a seat on the nearest couch, while Justin brought out the homework packet that his professor had assigned to him and his classmates.

She took a peek on what was to be done. The homework packet was filled with instructions that the professor had laid out, along with diagrams that he wanted them to finish. "Okay, let's take this one at a time. What topic are you having trouble with?"

Justin scratched his head. "I'm having trouble understanding whether this is an adjective or predicate adjective."

Maddie peered over his shoulder, looking at the sentence. *She thought the child spoiled.* She took a moment to think about it. "So, *she* is the subject, thought is the verb and *child* is the direct object."

He smiled. "You're actually explaining it better than my professor did," he complimented.

Feeling her cheeks begin to warm, she cleared her throat. "Thanks! So... I was thinking about the question you asked and while it does seem to be a regular adjective, it's a predicate adjective mainly because it's describing child but also completing the sentence."

Justin nodded. "That makes sense."

The two continued going through the homework packet, with Maddie feeling her confidence begin to grow at the thought of Justin's praise.

Chapter 7

The Long Road Ahead

Thursday, June 6, 2019

Maddie ran into Charlotte after a quiz in English class. Charlotte was one of her friends who used to work at Lakeview University's library reception desk in her college, and Maddie had never been happier. The two had met when she took an English class at Lakeview High, and from the moment they had agreed on how hard the course was at times, a beautiful friendship was formed.

She looked to her right, noticing her friend, Brian. He looked up to acknowledge her. "Hey, Maddie! What's up?"

Maddie shifted her weight from side to side. "Just need to borrow your friend for a minute here. I need to talk to her."

Brian frowned. "Is it about the order you're trying to get done for your friend's aunt? Just tell her that you need more time to make the delivery, nothing else to it."

Charlotte tapped her chin. "Oh yeah, Justin told me about that. He said you guys were going to try to make truffle filling this Friday, right?"

Maddie chuckled. "Thanks, Brian. But I can't move the date. That would just mess up everything Miss Caroline had planned." She turned her gaze back to Charlotte. "It's not really about that. I trust Justin to be patient with me."

Charlotte raised an eyebrow. "Then what is it?"

Maddie let out a deep breath she didn't know she was holding. "It's more of a personal matter. Can we talk?" She spared Brian an uneasy glance. "In private?"

Charlotte nodded. "Of course." She turned her head to the side, so she could let Maddie have some privacy.

"Hello?" she asked, waiting for Miss Caroline to talk.

"Hello, sweetie! I just wanted to make sure you got the description and picture of what type of decoration I want on the cake."

Maddie put Miss Caroline on hold, checking her messages to look at the cake. She blinked. *This wasn't what Miss Caroline wanted on the cake, was it?* There were two pictures. One of the New Year's Eve sparklers that people use to celebrate Fourth of July and various other holidays and another of a cake topper that was probably worth more than her allowance.

She tapped her phone's keyboard, resuming her call with Miss Caroline. "I mean no disrespect, ma'am. But... you sent me two pictures. Was that by mistake or?"

The other end was silent for a moment before Miss Caroline spoke. "Ah yes, I did, didn't I? I was going to ask you if you could do one teeny favor for me."

Maddie put on a fake smile, her grin stretching wider than usual. "Of course, what is it?"

"Do you think you could order that fancy cake topper and put it on the cake for me, please? Better yet, you could make it yourself. I know I said I wanted some sparklers, but I just changed the theme of my wedding from Independence Day to A Morning in Paris. Thank you! I'm looking forward to seeing how the cake turned out. Ta-ta!"

Maddie didn't even get a word in before Miss Caroline hung up on her. She looked at the phone, her breathing becoming labored again. She gripped the phone hard, wondering how Miss Caroline expected her to change something a few weeks before the wedding took place. The level of anxiety she felt became almost unbearable as her fingers started to tingle. She took deep breaths trying to calm herself down, only for that to make the feeling worse.

Moments like this were what triggered her anxiety in the first place. Whether it was because of something big or small, it was always there. She felt the walls begin to close in on her, trying to figure out a way to calm down. That was when Charlotte noticed her friend's disposition, leading her to a chair and trying to calm her down. "I know you're probably worried about what Miss Caroline said to you, but I know you can do this. Just try and think of your happy place like you told me to do, remember?"

Maddie nodded, before taking out her phone. She went to the Spotify app and played *In the Middle of Starting Over* by Sabrina Carpenter. The lyrics helped to calm her frenzied mind, feeling the anxiety slowly go away. A few minutes later, she took a few deep breaths before telling Charlotte what Miss Caroline had said.

Charlotte did a double-take. "She doesn't actually expect you to make that decoration, does she? She just dropped a bomb on you, and she knows it!"

Maddie bit her nails, feeling overwhelmed by the news.

Charlotte quickly noticed. "No, no, no. We'll have none of that, thank you," she said, like a parent softly scolding her child. "Now, since you've already agreed to make Miss

Caroline's wedding cake. You just have to figure out how you're going to price your cake since this is the first time you're doing something like this." She walked towards one of the college's computers, turning it on before entering her login details. At last, she motioned for Maddie to sit on the chair. "You might want to get comfortable. This is gonna take a while."

The brunette let out a frustrated groan, doing as she was told. She searched *wedding cake costs* on Google Chrome, hoping to find the answer she was looking for. Her eyes narrowed in on the first link, clicking on it. *Okay, let's see what we have here.* Her eyes scanned the page, reading the tips from top to bottom. Reaching for an unused notepad in her book bag, she jotted down the crucial facts, ranging from the cost of the wedding cake down to the decorations and small tray of desserts.

When she was done, Maddie handed the notepad to Charlotte, letting her see what she had written.

Charlotte nodded in approval as she went through everything Maddie had jotted down. "Okay, this is a good start. Now, do you have any free time today?"

Maddie pulled out her planner, going over the classes that she finished for today. She shook her head, smiling when she realized she had some time on her hands.

"Perfect! Now, let's get going to all your local bakeries and see how much they charge for their wedding cakes. Text your mom to let her know where you'll be going and the address," Charlotte directed. She gave Maddie a pointed stare. "You don't want your mom to worry about why you got home late."

Maddie shot her a bemused smile. "Ha-ha. Very funny."

The two friends got on the Panther Express bus, waving to the bus driver as they sat in their respective seats. Maddie looked out the window, awestruck with wonder at how there was so much to explore in the big city of Atlanta. It was just last week that Mia took her to this fantastic restaurant that served lamb gyros. *That was probably the best gyro she had ever tasted. Well, besides the one in New Orleans, that is.*

The two friends sat in silence until Charlotte spoke up. "So, what was it you wanted to tell me?"

Maddie looked around with a wary expression. There were too many people around to talk openly. She pointed to her phone and Charlotte nodded.

So, you know how I've been having trouble with college classes and everything? Maddie typed, sending the message to her.

A *ding* had alerted her that Charlotte had responded. *Yeah, what's up?*

Maddie typed at her phone's keyboard at lightning speed. *Well, I ended up going to my professors' office hours to ask him to explain things to me and it ended up helping a lot. My grades are much better than they were before.* She received a *ding* from her phone a few seconds later, smiling at Charlotte's response.

I'm so happy for you, girl. See? Asking for help is nothing to be ashamed of.

Maddie looked up from her phone, smiling in appreciation. She noticed a bakery with the logo saying *Warm Delights* on their storefront. "Excuse me, can you stop here, please?" she asked the bus driver, who put the vehicle to a halt as he allowed the girls to get off at their destination.

She and Charlotte walked into the bakery, seeing a young girl at the front of the cashier. "Welcome to *Warm Delights*. Are you looking for anything in particular?" the girl asked.

Maddie rubbed her shoulder, feeling nervous.

At that moment, she felt Charlotte lay a comforting hand on her shoulder. She nudged her arm. *Go on, I'll be right behind you if you need any help,* her warm expression conveyed.

The cashier gave Maddie a warm smile. "Hey, I remember you. You're one of my classmates in English class, right?"

She nodded, starting to remember the way that they used to talk before class.

"My name's Dana, also known as one of Charlotte's many friends," she greeted, then tapped her chin. "So, you're the famous Maddie that Charlotte speaks so highly of."

Maddie turned to look at Charlotte, who froze like a statue. Her thoughts started running amocko. *No, that's impossible. She would have known if Charlotte... Maybe she was reading too much into it. Just because Charlotte had a friendly personality didn't mean that she had feelings for her.* She struggled to get the words out. "She... she has?"

Dana nodded her head, giving Charlotte a sly grin. "Definitely. She always tells me how you've got a great work ethic when it comes to academics, not to mention that you're smart, beautiful–"

Charlotte gave her a dismissive wave. "Those are qualities I admire in any one of my friends." She narrowed her eyes at Dana. "Weren't you about to ask Maddie what she wanted?"

Dana shrugged. "Oh yeah, must have forgot."

Maddie turned to look at Charlotte, who was ready to throttle her classmate. She figured she better pick a dessert before Charlotte *completely* lost it. She looked at the display case, her eyes centered on one dessert. "Can I have the hummingbird cupcake, please?"

"Of course." Dana disappeared into the back, having a pair of gloves on when she came back out. She brought out the tray of cupcakes from the display case, putting one of them in a crinkly, brown bag. "That'll be $2.50. Anything else?"

"Yes, um, how much do you charge for your wedding cakes?" Maddie asked, her unease melting away as she became more confident now that she knew the girl.

Dana chewed her lip, walking into the back to get her boss.

An uncomfortable silence followed, with Maddie taking in Dana's words. She looked at Charlotte, who appeared unaffected by her comment.

When he came out, Maddie took in his appearance. The man had grey hair, with a beard running down the sides of his chin. His eyes looked tired, but the smile he sent her way told her that he loved his job and the employees who worked there.

"Hello, young lady. What can I do for you?" the man asked in a chipper tone.

"I wanted to ask how much you price your wedding cakes," Maddie replied, her answer bold and confident.

"We usually charge from around $200-$250. Why do you ask? You getting married or something?" the man asked with a chuckle.

Dana swatted her boss' arm. "That's personal, you goofball."

Maddie shook her head. "Oh no, this isn't for me. This is for my friend's aunt. I'm making a wedding cake for her, so I decided to ask around and see what local bakeries charge for their cakes. I was attracted to yours when I saw the fun sign," she explained, the thought of getting married surprising even her.

"Well, you're on the right track, miss. Keep up on the good work," The man commended, with him and Dana waving goodbye as they left the shop.

As Maddie and Charlotte continued their journey from shop to shop, Maddie couldn't help but think that finding out more information was just the beginning.

Chapter 8

The Art of Falling in Love

July 16, 2013

Six years earlier, Justin's best friend, Maddie, had decided to confess that she had feelings for him, but neither of them had expected the day to end on a sour note.

He and Maddie had an extra credit project to take care of, which required trying a new activity, so he had suggested that they watch the stars together in her backyard. There they were, surrounded by the darkness of the evening sky, the stars twinkling in the sky.

He looked up at the night sky, fascinated by it all.

"It's amazing how something as simple as a star can become so beautiful," Maddie thought aloud.

"Yeah, it really is," he contemplated, directing his gaze from the sky to his friend. He looked towards her, basking in the comfortable silence. "So... what are we supposed to do for our extra credit project?"

Maddie looked down at the paper her astronomy teacher gave them. "Well, according to this paper, we're supposed to write a paragraph about one aspect of astronomy we like and explain why."

"Sounds easy enough. What are you going to write about?" Justin asked, peering over at her paper.

She had given him a teasing grin. "That's a secret."

"Aw, come on... I thought we always told each other everything," he whined.

Maddie stuck her tongue out at him. "No, I tell my *girl*friends everything. You're a guy, so you're an exception to that rule."

Justin pouted. "Not funny, Mads."

She covered her mouth with her hand, trying to keep a straight face. "Well, for your information, I'm going to write about constellations."

Justin looked confused. "Specific ones or just in general?"

Maddie explained her answer. "In general. It would take a *pretty* long time to describe every single one, don't you think?"

He shrugged. "True."

She let out a deep breath. "By the way, there's something I've meant to ask you since we got here."

Justin stopped writing for a while. "Is it something bad?" he noticed that she was fidgeting with the purity ring she wore on her finger, a nervous habit she was prone to.

"Not... exactly," she trailed off.

Justin turned to her, looking at her dead in the face. "Okay, *now* you're starting to worry me. What's up, Mads?"

She had skidded her foot across the grass, her hands trembling from the raging emotions inside her.

He noticed this, giving her a concerned frown. "You okay? You're shaking."

She shrugged. "Yeah, I'm fine. Just a bit cold."

He took off his jacket and wrapped it around her, the shivering stopping as his arms wrapped around her. He should have known that the shivering was from nervousness since it was relatively cool that day.

"Thanks, but now you're going to be cold." She pouted.

He laughed. "I'm wearing a thick jacket underneath the sweater I gave you. If anything, you need it more than I do."

Maddie had looked towards the ground with a smile, taking a deep breath. She twisted a strand of hair in a circular motion to distract herself and began to feel an embarrassed blush color her cheeks. "I was just wondering... you called our time spent studying together a date while we were in class. Were you serious about that or... "

Justin bit his lip, trying to figure out the best way to go about this situation. He should have known this was coming sooner or later. While he did like hanging around her, he wasn't sure either of them was ready for a relationship right now. As the words tumbled out of her mouth, he felt an uncomfortable silence loom over the two of them. *Come on, say something, you idiot! And what? Try to pity her or, worse, dive headfirst into a relationship? That's not going to end well for either of you. Just be honest with her,* his mind rationed.

He continued to stay silent, knowing that Maddie was sensitive to these kinds of things. With her working on her bakery business, plus college classes, and him wanting to go to culinary school in four years, a relationship wasn't the best thing right now.

He winced, startled when he heard a bitter laugh come out of her mouth. "Well, I hope I didn't make our friendship awkward or anything."

Justin rubbed the back of his neck. "You didn't." He took a deep breath. "Here's the thing, Maddie. I know you like me, but if I'm speaking honestly, I don't know how *I* feel just yet. Plus, I don't think either of us is ready for a relationship right now, with you juggling college classes and running Creative Confections right now and me going to culinary school in a few months, I don't think things will work out."

Maddie turned away from him. "I understand."

He looked up from the ground, guilt making its way into his heart when he noticed a tear had run down the side of her cheeks. He needed to say something to salvage the situation. "But maybe someday soon." He meant it, hoping that when everything had settled down, he would be more open to starting a relationship with her and vice versa.

Someday. Maddie whispered the word to herself like it was magical. "I can work with that."

"Cool, so our friendship *isn't* shattered to bits?"

She laughed. "Of course not. I'll catch you later." The two sat in silence until her mom came to pick her up. He remembered the bittersweet smile she had on her face, trying to keep herself together.

He bit the inside of his cheek, kicking an aluminum Coca-Cola can that was on the grass. *Their friendship may not be shattered, but he doubted that it would ever go back to the way it was.*

Chapter 9

Strength in Numbers

Wednesday, June 12, 2019

Maddie hopped around the bakery shop, ready to get started with the next recipe she and Justin were going to make. She walked up towards him, maintaining eye contact. "We're making mint chocolate chip cupcakes. Is that okay?"

"Sounds good to me," Justin said. He let out a chuckle, a smile tugging at his lips, showing her the video on his phone.

She tapped the arrow under the video, causing the list of the items to appear at her fingertips. "Let's see, we need flour, granulated sugar, cocoa powder, baking soda, chocolate chips, salt... " Maddie trailed off, reading the list of ingredients her idol put in the description of the video.

As Justin listed the ingredients, she poured each component into the mixing bowl, making sure that she measured each ingredient correctly. Her eyes drifted from the bowl, outside toward the storefront. The words on her bakery's window caught her eye as she started pouring the salt. Ignoring the falling grains, she squinted her eyes to see the message. She felt her heart stop with overwhelming memories once she made out the graffiti sitting on the window pane. *Justin's only hanging out with you because of the perks he could get. Your bakery is picking up off the ground, and you're finally raking in cash. Who wouldn't want those benefits?*

The bullying had occurred ten years ago. Maddie had just gotten used to her new school. Her teachers liked her, she was making new friends, things seemed like they were falling into place. Then disaster reared its ugly head. One of the downsides to being popular was that there were always people who got jealous when they saw you succeeding. That was the case when one of the girls decided to trip Maddie, making her spill her lunch.

Things started to get worse once she told the principal, who decided to give all the girls detention for their punishment. She remembered the cold, calculating looks each of them gave her, warning her that she would pay for it one day. She just didn't know that day would be today. Word probably spread fast about her being the one to make Miss Caroline's wedding cake. She had a hunch that the girls were a few of those people, who, when overhearing the news, were probably jealous of her.

They were probably fuming over how Maddie had success over her bakery business while they were still in the same place they were a few years ago.

"Maddie? Maddie! Maddie, snap out of it!"

Maddie shook her head, Justin's voice snapping her out of her thoughts. She looked at him, her heart thumping in her chest. His brow was creased, and his mouth pressed into a straight line.

"Is everything okay?" he questioned.

She plastered a smile on her face. "Yeah, why do you ask?"

"Oh, I don't know. Maybe because you poured a lot of salt into the mix instead of a *fourth* of a teaspoon," Justin responded in a deadpan tone.

Maddie fidgeted with her fingers, looking down at the mess she created. "Damn it!" she shouted, wondering why she made such a careless mistake.

Justin grabbed her hands. "Hey, hey, it's okay. I'm sure it doesn't taste that bad," he reassured her.

"Please don't–" she started, but it was too late as he took a spoon to taste the creation before them.

His lips twisted into a grimace, clearing his throat as he looked down at Maddie. "A little salty, but–"

"Sorry," Maddie muttered. She tried to put on a smile. "Hope you don't mind if we take a quick break." She walked over the dining table, angry at herself for getting distracted over something so small.

She stayed silent, trying to stop the tears from rolling down her cheek. The "anonymous" graffiti she had just read caused the tears to flow. She knew that the words weren't true, *so... why did those words bother her like they did?* Maddie wished Justin didn't have to see her like this. She hated being so vulnerable.

"Really, it's okay... " he pleaded, ushering her to a chair to sit on. He looked toward the storefront, following where her gaze once was. The graffiti written on one of the bakery's windows caught his attention as he went outside to tear it off from the window. His curiosity outweighed the rational part of his brain, tearing his gaze from the storefront to the words spray-painted on the front window.

He turned his gaze towards her, walking over to her with a chair in his hands. "Sorry, didn't mean to scare you."

Maddie tucked a strand of hair behind her ear. "It's okay. It's best if you hear what happened to me before you hear it from someone else."

The two friends were silent for a moment before Justin opened his mouth to speak. "You don't have to tell me if you don't want to, you know. I'm not obligated to know anything."

She shook her head. "I know, but... I want to." She took a deep breath, decided that she trusted him enough to tell him the whole story and that nothing would leave this room.

Justin formed a grin. "Whenever you're ready."

Maddie took some deep breaths before she started to talk. "You already know that I used to get bullied in sixth grade when I started public school. It didn't really matter much since my friend Aiden was there to help me during that time." She stared into the distance. "but what you don't know is how severe the bullying became."

He clenched his fingers. "Oh... "

She sucked in a deep breath, with Justin rubbing her back. "I should have watched where I was going. If I had, I would have seen one of the girls had purposely stuck her foot out to trip me."

Maddie smiled. "After I turned fourteen, my mom decided to put me in private school up until college. I'm glad that she made that call, but at the same time, life would have been a whole lot better if I didn't have to go through that." She stayed silent, looking at the tissue in her lap and throwing it towards the trash can. "I guess I was a bit naive, thinking I wouldn't experience bullying because I was different," she said, putting air quotes around the word, different.

"You're not. Being different is awesome! Well, it is for me, anyway. I always liked your signature pigtails."

Justin's words hadn't sunk in yet as Maddie kept talking a mile a minute. "I remember a boy who stayed with me for a while, making sure I was okay after the incident. He gave me a hug, telling me everything was gonna be okay. The chocolates he decided to give me helped too." She took a look at Justin again, realizing that he looked like the same boy that she had made friends with that day. The realization suddenly dawned on her.

She opened her mouth in shock, pointing her finger at him. "Wait a minute, that was you?!"

He scratched the back of his head. "Guilty," he managed to get out.

Maddie squealed, reaching out her arms to give him a hug. "Thank you! You have no idea how much that moment meant to me." Catching on to what she did, she retracted her hands, her cheeks growing warm at her forwardness.

Justin softly grabbed her hand, kissing the back of it. "Now, what kind of person would I have been if I had left you by yourself? You looked like you could've used a friend, so I decided *hey, why not?*" he teased, a smile tugging at his lips.

Maddie broke eye contact with him, her eyes looking up at the ceiling. "I remember you also told me to tell you something about myself, so I decided to tell you how I started learning Japanese after my library canceled the anime clubs I used to go to when I was younger." Her eyes sparkled in excitement. "You let me practice my Japanese with you for a few minutes."

He blinked, surprised that she had remembered something that happened a long time ago. "No problem." He held her gaze, moving closer toward her. "If I remember right, your Japanese sounded really pretty too." He laid a hand on her shoulder. "And don't worry about those girls. You won't have to worry when your knight in shining armor is around. Not to say you can't stand up for yourself, though." He got up from his chair, stretching out his hand towards hers. "Now, let's get back to baking, shall we, mademoiselle?"

Maddie's lips grinned. "We shall."

The two went back to making the cake, but not before cleaning up the graffiti that the girls had left on the bakery's window. The thought of Justin having her back during that moment, and even now, caused her heart to flutter in a way she never thought was possible.

Chapter 10

Awkward Moments All Around

Thursday, June 13, 2019

Justin whistled a tune to himself as he walked into the doors of the college library. His blood boiled at the thought of yesterday's events as the image of Firecracker crying came to mind. *Why people choose to be mean to each other was beyond him.* He walked up to his friend, Charlotte, as they exchanged a hug. "Hey, Charlotte. How's it going?"

She lifted her gaze from the computer to where he was standing. "Going well, thanks. Just trying to figure out how I'm going to work on this assignment. I'm supposed to be seeing my friend today."

He arched an eyebrow. "Who's your friend?"

She pointed to a girl who just walked through the sliding doors. "Her."

He turned around, his eyes widening when he turned his gaze toward the door. Maddie walked inside the library, wearing a trendy checkered top with light blue jeans that complimented her figure.

Charlotte waved to her, motioning for her to come over to say hi. He couldn't help but admire Maddie as she walked closer toward him. *Wow, she looks beautiful...* He could feel himself sweating bullets as she moved closer and closer into his line of sight.

"Lottie!" Maddie exclaimed, rushing up to give her friend a tight hug.

He noticed Charlotte smile at Maddie's enthusiasm. "Huh, never heard of that nickname before."

Maddie fidgeted with the purity ring on her finger, stammering. "Sorry, I didn't mean to offend you. I can call you Charlotte if you want... "

"I never said I didn't like it," Charlotte interjected with a teasing glint in her eyes.

She gave her a small laugh. "I knew that."

The two girls stayed silent for a moment before Maddie noticed him. "Oh, hey, Justin. I didn't see you there."

He gave her a blanched look. *Are you kidding me?*

"Not that you're invisible or anything. I just haven't seen Lottie in a while so–"

Justin waved off her nervous rambling. "No worries, Firecracker. No harm done." He paused for a moment. "Wait a minute. Are we talking about the same person here? Because if we are, she's the friend I mentioned who supported me in culinary school."

"No way. That's so cool!"

Charlotte rubbed the back of her neck. "It was nothing."

Maddie's eyes widened in disbelief. "It wasn't nothing. You helped Justin when he needed it, and for that, thanks."

"You're welcome. By the way, I didn't see you at the library yesterday. Everything okay?"

Maddie rubbed her arm, softly grabbing Charlotte's hand and motioning for them to go sit down at a table to talk things over. Charlotte followed her lead, telling him they'd be right back.

She probably wants to tell her what happened yesterday. Justin figured. He walked closer to them, interested in hearing their conversation. Hiding under the table in front of them so he wouldn't get caught, he carried on.

The two exchange words with one another, with Charlotte exclaiming, "They did what?!"

Maddie shushed her. "Let the whole school hear you, why don't ya?"

Charlotte winced. "Sorry, but I can't believe they did something like that. Can't you like, report it to the college or something?"

The brunette waved it off. "It's okay. Justin made me feel better, anyway."

Justin watched Maddie rest her chin in the palm of her hands, looking to the side.

"Someone has a crush," Charlotte sang.

Justin froze.

Maddie plopped her hands onto the table. "What? No, I don't."

"You do. You absolutely do," Charlotte sang again.

"Don't be ridiculous. Besides, I have the bakery and college to focus on. I have no time for guys, much less a relationship." Maddie argued.

Charlotte raised an eyebrow. "If you say so."

Maddie stayed silent for a moment, contemplating what had happened before today. "By the way, about what Dana said... "

Charlotte shifted her feet a little. "You know Dana was just joking, right? Why wouldn't I talk about someone as awesome as yourself?" She let out a snort. "You're pretty easy to talk to and Dana was right about you being beautiful. However, that doesn't mean that I swing that way though." She darted her eyes from left to right, making sure no one was listening. "One of my coworkers works in the library across from our university. He's really cute like you wouldn't believe!" She looked in Justin's direction, narrowing her eyes at the nearby table he was hiding under. "Justin, come out here right now! Don't *make* me have to kick your ass."

Crap! Justin slowly got up, seeing the look of horror written across Maddie's face. "You were listening in?"

"Only for a little bit," he reassured her, noticing Maddie's heated glare.

Charlotte raised an eyebrow, causing him to cave.

"Okay, fine!" He turned away from the two girls, feeling the heat radiating off of them. "I listened to the rest of your conversation. Sorry. But in my defense, you were talking out in the open, so I figured that only part of your conversation was private."

"So was the rest of it, fool!" Charlotte slapped him upside the head.

"Ow!" He rubbed the back of his head. "I guess I deserved that."

He continued to watch the conversation between his friends go on, the feeling of being left out making its way inside his chest. *He guessed it was true what people said: three was definitely a crowd.*

Charlotte tapped her chin. "Oh, and I meant to thank you for helping me with my homework the other day."

Maddie turned her gaze away from her, fidgeting with her purity ring. "I try, plus I figured that if I could finish the homework, why not help someone else with it?"

Charlotte laid a hand on her shoulder. "That makes sense."

He nodded his head. "Mhmm. By the way, are you feeling any better since yesterday?"

"Yeah, thanks for being there when I needed it."

"You're welcome. I'd do anything for a friend," Justin said, realizing his *very* poor choice of words. He watched Maddie's smile twist into a confused frown while Charlotte slapped her head with a resounding *smack!*

"Not that you're just a friend. You're like one of the guys. No, you are *not* a guy..." he rambled, trying to figure out how to get out of the hole he dug for himself.

Maddie quirked an eyebrow and smiled.

"Boys... " Charlotte muttered to herself, turning her attention back to the computer in front of her.

He tugged at the collar of his shirt. "Is it getting hot in here, or is it just me?"

"Nope, just you," Charlotte said with an expressionless look.

"Thank you, Charlotte," Justin said with gritted teeth. *Why did he think to tell her about his crush on Maddie again?*

She promised not to tease him about it, she said. She would be on his side, she said... Justin muttered under his breath, wondering why he was friends with Charlotte in the first place.

He watched as Maddie waved back to him and Charlotte, running to her next class.

Charlotte stood behind him, shaking her head. "In the twenty-two years of my life, I have never felt that embarrassed to be friends with you," she commented, walking back to the library's reception desk to continue her shift.

Chapter 11

A New Revelation

Saturday, June 15, 2019

Justin sat in front of his laptop, trying to figure out what his professor wanted him and his classmates to do for his creative writing assignment. He had a basic understanding of it but struggled to comprehend how he should go about writing it. Taking a break from the work he had done (or started anyway), he took out his photo album to look at all the pictures he, Charlotte, and Maddie had taken over the years.

There was one picture that stood out among the rest, the day he had left for his flight to culinary school: Maddie looked surprised as he had kissed the top of her forehead, giving her a warm look afterward. It was one of the somewhat bittersweet memories that occurred throughout that year.

* * *

*Two years ago, on **Friday, January 6, 2017**, he was planning to leave for his trip when the thought of her made its way into his thoughts. It would have been a shame if* *he left for culinary school without saying a word to her, so he decided to call her on Skype.*

He dragged his feet from the table to his bed, bringing his laptop along with him. His eyes drifted to Maddie's name, taking a deep breath before he pressed the call button.

Two rings later, Maddie's face appeared on the screen. Her dark, brown hair looked messy as she ran her fingers through it, trying to smooth out the edges to make it as neat as possible.

"You know it's only me, right? You look beautiful, no matter what."

She fidgeted, grabbing her teddy bear to cuddle. "I know... it's just... " She shook her head. "Never mind that, how's packing for culinary school going?"

"Going well, my flight leaves at one in the afternoon, so I'm driving there early due to traffic."

She gave him a small smile. "Wouldn't want you to miss your flight."

He gave her a short nod. "Yeah, wish I were an early morning person like you, though. Would make driving there much easier."

"Being a morning person isn't all it's cracked up to be. My internal clock wakes

me up at odd hours of the morning. Like three a.m. early."

He chuckled. "But you like waking up early because it gives you a chance to watch the sunrise."

She zoned out like she was trying to remember something. "It reminds me of my first vacation in Canada. When my family and I stayed at my aunt's house, I used to get up every day by my window and watch the sunrise. Then later, I would sit in front of the TV and watch Anne of Green Gables."

She rested her chin in the palm of her hands, reminiscing about the good, old days.

He smiled sadly. "Sorry, you had to end up moving, though. Can't imagine what they would have been like." He maintained eye contact with her. "What was life like back in the UK?

Maddie's eyes lit up, a certain kind of sparkle in them. "Well, it's sometimes rainy there, but there are days when there's sunshine as well. My mom and I used to have these cookies that we loved to buy while living there. Some things are cheaper here than here in the U.S. and the last time I went there was for my aunt's wedding. It was so much fun! My grandma tried to make me dance at my aunt's wedding." She covered her face with her hands. "It was a little embarrassing, but we had a lot of fun." She took a peek behind her hands, noticing that he was laughing.

Maddie stuck her nose in the air but turned to look at her screen. She stuck her tongue out at him. "But anyways, don't be sorry that I ended up moving here. Meeting you was one of the best things that has ever happened to me." She bit her lip, turning her head to the side. "You made me feel welcomed, and I appreciate that."

He looked away from the screen, clearing his throat. "No problem, Cupcake."

She squinted her eyes at the screen, moving her face closer so that she could see him clearly. "Valdez, are you blushing?"

"D-d-don't be ridiculous," he stammered.

"Oh my gosh, you totally are. That's so adorable."

"Shut up," he muttered.

She held in her laughter. "Well, it's getting late, so I'll text you before your flight tomorrow."

He waved. "Goodnight, Firecracker."

Maddie looked taken back, trying to compose herself.

He gave her a lopsided grin. "Now, who's the flustered one?"

She rolled her eyes. "Goodnight, Justin," she persisted, determined not to let him have the last laugh.

She logged off before he could tease her any further, causing him to smile to himself.

He laid his head on the pillow, thinking about all the times they spent together. Everything about her, her light-brown skin, her captivating brown eyes, her smile. Any one of those things always drew Justin to her, like a moth akin to a flame. He frowned, not liking the direction his thoughts were heading to. He groaned into his pillow, punching his fist into it quietly. This was definitely bad timing. Why did now have to be the day when he realized his feelings for Maddie?

He soon found himself at Hartsfield-Jackson Airport the next morning, his attention turning to a man who looked at his watch, then raced down the hall to the main entrance. The airport was packed with people either waiting for their loved ones to come home or rushing to catch an early morning flight. He dreamed of arriving at the front of Silver Oak Institute of Fine Arts, being surrounded by people of his kind, working towards the same goal of becoming a pastry chef.

Justin looked back at the group of people who came to see him off. He first noticed his mom, dabbing her tears away with a napkin, then his dad, who was trying to put on a tough front for his mom.

"I'm gonna miss you guys," he said, wrapping his arms around the people who had raised him to be the man he was today.

Amber stuck her tongue out at him, holding up a sign that read, "I'll miss you too, not!" Justin shook his head. Typical Amber. Always finding a way to make even the most serious of moments funny as hell.

"I'm gonna miss you, Blondie," he joked as Amber narrowed her eyes at him.

"Don't call me that," she replied as Justin enveloped her in a hug.

Finally, his eyes landed on Maddie, who decided to wear something special for the occasion. She wore a solid button front corduroy dress on top of a plain, long-sleeve white top, managing to pull off the look effortlessly. He always liked Maddie's sense of style, even though Mia was the outfit guru between the two sisters.

He walked back to the group, giving each of them a hug before stopping short of Maddie. There were so many things that he wanted to say, but the words died down on his lips the second he looked at her.

Justin sighed before giving Maddie a tight hug. "I think I'm going to miss you most of all," he whispered into her ear.

Maddie held back tears as she hugged him tighter, never wanting to let go. "You better make sure you call me or else the next time you come home, you'll end up with a broken wrist."

"I'll hold you to that, Firecracker," he said in a low tone only meant for her to hear.

Maddie sniffed while Justin's heart ached for the girl who he would be miles away from. An idea popped into his mind. It would make for a bittersweet goodbye, but he wanted to make her happy.

"You better go before you miss your flight," her voice broke at the thought of the two being so far apart.

"I will, but not before I do this," he said, planting a soft kiss on her forehead. A slow smile came across Maddie's face as she melted into the hug, savoring the moment.

The two broke apart before Justin looked at her to gauge her reaction. She was glowing from head to toe, the smile she wore on her face making him as happy as she was.

Justin waved goodbye to others shortly before he boarded the plane. As he fastened his seatbelt, a young woman tapped him on the shoulder. He turned toward her, recognizing the person beside him. "Charlotte?" This wasn't the Charlotte he knew from Lakeview High. She wore a long-sleeved, orange tie-dye top with mid-length shorts and a black jacket to match. He guessed she was going for a casual, but confident look.

After what seemed like an uncomfortable silence that looked like it went on for way too long, Charlotte spoke. "Are you just going to keep staring at me, or are we gonna have a conversation, dude?"

Justin chuckled. "Sorry, it's just been so long since I've seen you."

"Well, we have some time to kill. So, what's been going on?"

As Justin and Charlotte talked, he had a feeling that culinary school was going off to a great start.

* * *

He recalled the memory with a sad smile, shaking his head in disbelief, wondering where all the time had gone. Having realized that his feelings for Maddie had grown since then, he felt stumped. He needed to confide to someone about this, but who?

Chapter 12

A Pinkie Promise

Monday, June 17, 2019

Justin laid down on his bed, thinking of all the events that had triggered his feelings towards Maddie. He remembered one day when they had started their senior year of high school.

* * *

On **Friday, January 10, 2014**, *Justin could feel the cool* breeze as *he and many other students had just walked out of his last class, his feet shuffling across the marble floor of Lakeview High. He had put his hands in his pockets, whistling the tune of Rude by MAGIC. Lifting his head up for a moment, he saw Maddie talking to some people while she sat on a chair against the classroom door.*

Watching her, he noticed that she tended to cover her mouth when she laughed, afraid that someone would see how awkward she was. He shook his head, wondering why she valued people's opinions so much and hoped she would eventually grow out of it. Admiring her from afar, he watched her use her hand to motion to come and join her.

He chuckled, walking toward her and her posse. "Hey, Mads! What's up?"

She shrugged. "Nothing much, we were just talking about what we were going to do over spring break."

He looked at her friends up and down, trying to sort out if they were people he knew. The first person he recognized among his group of friends was Charlotte, shaking her long, black braided hair as she nodded her head towards what was being said. "I see you've already met Charlotte," he commented.

Maddie turned her gaze toward him. "Yeah, she introduced herself to me, and we just started chatting."

His glance turned to another friend beside her, laughing. He was probably Maddie's best friend from high school.

Dusting herself off, Maddie excused herself from her friends. "I'll be right back."

As she turned around, Justin noticed that there was a dark, red spot on her jeans that hadn't been there before. He rushed to her aid, pulling her aside.

"Hey! What gives?" she exclaimed, looking at him with a frown.

He leaned in towards her, the close contact making him nervous. He couldn't just allow her to embarrass herself like this.

Her frown turned into a look of concern. "Justin, what's wrong? You're scaring me."

"Your pants..." he trailed off. "Your pants are stained red," he whispered into her ear.

She let out a gasp, her eyes darting from side to side. "This can't be happening. This can't be happening..." she muttered to herself.

"Just calm down. I'll walk you towards the bathroom so you can change."

He guided her towards the girl's bathroom, his body hiding the stained pants from anyone's view. He put his hand near her lower back, feeling her flinch.

"Watch it, buddy," he heard her warn.

He sighed. "Sorry, but it's spreading."

Walking toward the nearest bathroom, Maddie walked away with her head down. It was the first time he had to help her with something like this.

He looked up, feeling someone's gaze on him and smiled when he saw that Maddie was watching him. She smiled, getting what looked like a small paper airplane from her pocket. Letting the paper go, he watched it soar into the air and land at his feet.

Reading the message it contained, Justin was amazed at her neat handwriting. He had never seen a note written in cursive before. "Thanks for helping a girl out," he read, looking up in her direction.

He winked at her, causing her to cover her face in embarrassment.

Thirty minutes later, Justin had walked toward her with a long dress paired with short leggings in his hands. "While we were on our two-hour break, I asked my mom to get you some clothes from the shopping mall near our school. Hope you don't mind."

"Thank you, Justin," she said, taking the clothes from him with gratitude.

"You'll find something you might need hiding in the clothes," he continued.

He remembered the flustered look on her face when she saw

what was hidden in the clothes. "Thanks," she mumbled, looking away. "You promise not to tell anyone?"

He intertwined his pinkie with hers. "Pinkie promise."

A few feet away, he saw Charlotte talking to a boy, twirling her hair in a rather poor attempt to look flirty. "I'll be right back."

He walked over to Charlotte, pulling her away from the boy. "She'll be right back."

Justin rolled his eyes as she protested the entire time, causing a few heads to turn their way. "I'm not getting paid enough for this," he muttered under his breath.

The two went to where Maddie was standing, looking a bit uncomfortable. "Thank you, Justin, for dragging me away from what could have been the most important conversation of my life," Charlotte got out while gritting her teeth.

He gave her a dismissive wave. "You'll have other chances to talk to Romeo. We got a situation here."

She crossed her arms. "What kind of situation?"

He coughed, turning his gaze over to Maddie. "Code red."

Maddie softly giggled, covering her hands with her mouth to conceal it. "Only you would choose to make a pun in a serious situation, Skyscraper."

Justin moved closer to her. "Skyscraper. I like it! Only because you made it very clear that I'm three inches taller than you," he boasted, wearing a proud smile on his face.

Maddie's grin slowly turned to a pout. "Meanie."

Charlotte tapped her foot. "Okay, I'm completely lost here. What happened that's so important?" she asked.

Justin explained the situation to Charlotte, causing her to wince in sympathy.

She turned to Maddie. "I'm so sorry, Maddie," she whispered.

"It's okay. Justin brought me some new clothes, although I have yet to see if they fit."

Maddie was about to go to the bathroom when she noticed him gesture to Charlotte.

"That's what I brought Charlotte for, Firecracker. I brought her here so she could see if the clothes fit."

Charlotte looked at the clothes, giving Justin a quick glance. "I gotta admit, I'm surprised. Never expected you to have good taste in clothes."

Justin scowled. "Thanks... I think."

She ushered Maddie towards the bathroom, making sure she was situated before closing the door behind her. She turned to give Justin a side-eye. "You like her," she teased.

He scoffed, turning his head away. "No, I don't. She's just a good friend."

Charlotte let out a long, exasperated sigh. "Whatever, just... let me know how much I owe you for the clothes."

He waved his hand. "Don't worry about it."

"You sure?"

"Of course. Besides, Maddie needed my help, and I wouldn't be a friend if I didn't try to help her, right?"

"Whipped," Charlotte loudly coughed out.

"Am not!" he argued back.

The boy who was with them earlier quickly walked up to them. "I hate to disagree with you, man, but... " He laid a comforting hand on his shoulder. "I have to agree with Charlotte. That was a pretty cool thing to do."

Justin shoved the boy's arm away. "Get your arm off me before you lose it," he warned, his frown turning into a pout.

After she got done changing, Maddie came back into the hallways to find Lottie and Justin locked in a staring contest. She looked between the two of them. "So... what's up?"

Charlotte turned to Maddie with a lopsided grin. "I was just telling Justin that he-"

"Has a surprise for you!" Justin finished, with Charlotte giving him a wtf look.

Confused at the change in his tone, Maddie tilted her head sideways. "You do?"

He looked to Charlotte, who shook her head. "Sorry, dude, you're on your own with this one."

Justin looked back at Maddie, who had a doe-eyed expression on her face.

* * *

Justin had only said what he said because he didn't want Charlotte to put him in an awkward situation. He sighed, tossing and turning in his bed. He still hadn't found someone to talk to about his crush. A few hours later, he quickly texted Charlotte. *Hey. Do you think we can meet up at the library tomorrow? It's important. Just promise that you won't make fun of me.*

A beep from his phone had alerted him that she had texted back. He unlocked his screen, his eyes adjusting to the bright light before seeing the message. *I promise. Now, where do you want to meet up?*

Chapter 13

A Heart to Heart Talk

Tuesday, June 18, 2019

Justin looked at his watch, wondering when Charlotte was going to get here. *Where is she?*

Ten minutes later, she rushed through the doors of the library, panting as she got to the table he was sitting at.

"Sorry I'm late. I had a math test that took me *forever* to finish."

Justin waved his hand. "No problem. I wasn't waiting long."

She smiled. "That's good. So, what's up?"

"I have a crush on Maddie," he muttered.

"What was that? I couldn't quite hear you," she teased, moving her ear closer so that she could hear him.

Justin gritted his teeth. "You know damn well you heard me."

She threw her head back, laughing. "I'm just teasing you, dude."

He turned away from her, muttering something incoherent.

"Anyway, so you have a crush on Maddie. What are you going to do about it?"

He started tapping his foot on the ground, the idea of deciding now paralyzing him. Charlotte put a hand on his knee, stopping the thumping for a while. "No, no, there will be none of that while I'm around. I know the very thought of telling Maddie how you feel scares you, and that's okay. We're all scared to do things at one point or another, but life's too short not to take any risks."

Justin pondered her words for a moment, letting them sink in. *Taking risks, huh?*

"But what if she doesn't feel the same way?" he reasoned.

She gave him a small smile. "Then at least you know. It's better than not knowing."

"I don't know, things might get worse... might as well come up with a plan, what if—"

"Or... " she interjected. "She could feel the same way, and you guys could live happily ever after."

Justin gave her a blank stare.

"Look, it's good to calculate the pros and cons of situations, but you can't go through life thinking 'what if'."

He gave her a long sigh, wondering what he should do. Thoughts raced through his head a mile a minute as he thought of the last time he worked with Maddie.

* * *

The day before, he walked into Creative Confections, watching Maddie as she brought out each ingredient and laid it out on the table to see. "What are you making, Firecracker?"

She looked up from what she was doing, startled from the sudden voice. "Justin, you scared me."

"Not my fault you scare so easily," he teased.

Maddie rolled her eyes at him, continuing with the task at hand.

"So, what are you making this time?" Justin piped up.

Maddie grinned. "I'm making blueberry crumble cupcakes. It's one of the first recipes my favorite baker ever made, so I wanted to try it out. It's a cake recipe, but I'm turning it into cupcakes since that seems more fun." she explained.

Watching the video on her phone, Justin watched in admiration as Maddie's eyes twinkled from the excitement of watching her favorite baker.

As she started pouring the ingredients into the bowl one by one, Justin came towards where she was.

"What are you doing?" she asked, running a hand through her hair.

"Trying to help."

"Thanks, but I don't need your help."

He put a hand over his heart. "You wound me."

Maddie snorted, getting back to mixing the ingredients together.

Justin stood to the side, admiring the way she was so focused. "Well, I see you have it under control, so I'll just be going then." As he spun around to leave, Maddie softly grabbed his arm.

"Please don't leave," she said a moment later.

He turned back, looking at her face as she gave him the most adorable puppy dog look known to mankind. This girl was going to be the death of him. She just had to give him that look, didn't she?

He thought about it for a moment. "Are your parents home?"

Maddie looked back at him before putting the cupcakes in the oven. "Yeah, I called them while you were busy drooling over the cupcakes I was making."

He turned away and groaned, trying to find something to distract himself with. Was it that obvious?

She let out a chuckle. "It's okay. You're not the only one who likes taking little tastes of what they make, and I don't know why I told you that."

Justin snorted, a laugh threatening to escape his lips.

She walked back to the table, finding the white kitchen timer, and twisting it to the desired number of minutes the cupcakes needed to bake for.

While they waited for the cupcakes, Maddie walked from the tabletop to the fridge, opening it. She rummaged through the fridge, smiling when she found the object she desired. She pulled out two sandwiches wrapped in parchment paper, placing one in front of Justin.

"Wanted to offer you something to eat since you're my guest and everything. You must be hungry."

His stomach growled, proving her point. He turned his head to the side, looking anywhere but her. "Maybe."

Maddie chuckled as they ate their sandwiches in silence.

Before they knew it, the timer rang, signaling that the cupcakes were done.

Sticking a toothpick in each cupcake, Justin noticed something unusual about them. "Why only six?"

"I decided to half the recipe so nothing would be wasted," Maddie explained.

He tapped his chin. "So, what are you going to do with the rest?" It would be a shame if the cupcakes were to go to waste.

Maddie thought about it for a moment. "Mmm, probably give some to my classmates."

Justin blinked. "You're taking summer classes?"

She turned her gaze to see Justin looking at her for an explanation. "I need to if I wanna graduate on time. It isn't fun, but I try to enjoy the experience."

Justin smiled. "That's good. How are they going so far?"

Maddie groaned. "Other than feeling like I'm going to collapse from working on this group project, it's going pretty well."

Justin looked taken back. "It isn't that bad... is it?"

"No... " she hesitated.

He gave her a pointed look.

"Sometimes, I end up doing the most work and taking responsibility when something goes wrong," she blurted out.

Justin opened his mouth to say something, but she put a hand up.

"I know I shouldn't feel like I have to do everything, but my grade depends on this, Justin!" she emphasized, running a hand from her hair.

He knew that was a sign that she was upset and frowned. "How are you guys graded on the group presentation?"

"Oh, we're graded as a team," Maddie replied.

Justin grit his teeth. Group projects weren't fun, especially when they were graded that way. If someone didn't pull their weight in the project, the entire team suffered. "Man, that sucks."

"Tell me about it," she said, putting the cupcakes on a cooling rack.

"But at least I have the bakery to look forward to... " Maddie kicked the imaginary dirt with her foot, turning her attention from the cupcakes to her partner in crime. "And hanging out with you, of course," she added.

He snorted. "Well, it's nice to know that you like my company, even if I was an afterthought."

* * *

Justin turned his attention back to Charlotte. "I'll think about it," he decided.

"That's all I could ask for," she relented, getting up from her seat.

Justin followed suit, stretching his arms as he did so.

Waving goodbye to her, he walked out of the library, feeling like he was ready for anything life threw at him.

Chapter 14

A Cozy Afternoon

Wednesday, June 19, 2019

Maddie ran down the stairs as she heard the doorbell ring. "Coming!" she yelled out, running toward the bathroom mirror first, fixing her hair and clothes, making sure she looked decent enough for the person who was waiting on the other side of the door. She peered through the front window, surprised to see *him* on the other side. "Justin? Not that I'm *not* happy to see you, but what's going on?"

"I've already asked your parents, so I'm taking you out to a local coffee shop that I think you might enjoy. It was on the list of the Atlanta magazine."

She gave him a side-eye. "Well, if you say so. Just let me change into something nice and call my parents."

"I'll be waiting." He gave her a smile as he went into the car and shut the door behind him.

Running upstairs, she clasped her hands behind her back. *Justin wanted to hang out with her*. She blinked. Wait, did her mom already know about this? Maddie had a feeling she did. She dialed her mom's number. "Hey, Mom. Did you arrange for me to hang out with Justin this afternoon?"

She heard her mom snap her fingers on the other end. "Oh, yes. Now I remember. I know that you have a deadline and everything, but you've been working so hard that I thought you could use a break."

Maddie took a long, deep breath. "And you didn't think to ask me first?" she asked in a clipped tone.

"Don't use that tone with me, young lady. We've talked about this," her mother scolded.

Maddie looked down at the ground, feeling a bit guilty. "Sorry, Mom, but a heads up would have been nice."

"I know, Sweetie. I'm sorry too. But you've already showered and everything. Now you just have to find something to wear."

Maddie groaned. "But that's the hard part."

Her mother laughed. "I'll be praying for you, sweetie. Love you and see you later."

Maddie ended the call feeling a bit lighter but still guilty. *She really needed to work on controlling her temper.*

Going through each outfit in her closet, her eyes stopped at a simple, green, checkered dress that looked perfect for the occasion. She sighed, singing *When He Sees Me* to herself.

Maddie hummed the rest of the lyrics to herself, smoothing out her dress with her hands.

Justin honked the horn of his car, causing her to jump a foot in the air. *Boys... so impatient sometimes.*

She looked herself over once more, her springy curls bouncing near the side of her head. "Bye, Clara. I'm off to hang out with Justin," she called out, hearing a sad *meow* in response. She had better remind her sister to play with her once she and mom get back from shopping.

Maddie locked the door behind, shaking her arms to get the nerves off her. *Why the hell was she so nervous? It's just Justin.* She stepped inside the front seat of the car, shutting the door after her. "Hey, Justin. Sorry, I kept you waiting."

She turned to see him with his mouth ajar. "Wanna take a picture? It will last longer."

Justin snapped out of his stupor, directing his gaze to the window. "Sorry, I just... you clean up well."

"You're not so bad, yourself, I guess."

He huffed. "You... guess?"

Maddie snorted. "Wouldn't want to inflate your ego *too* much."

"You're something else entirely, Jones."

She rubbed her arm. "Is... is that a bad thing?"

Justin locked eyes with her. "In this situation, not at all."

She turned away from him, feeling her cheeks heat up.

The pair drove down the road, with Maddie looking out the window to see birds soaring through the air. A car's horn shattered the peaceful view. "Traffic is really bad. It might take us a while," Justin piped up.

Google maps showed long red lines in every direction heading to the city. Cars lined up as a cat usually stretches out, long and lazy. Peering inside some of the vehicles, Maddie could see people getting frustrated. Sneaking into lanes, the drivers honked their horns, testing Justin's impatience.

Thirty minutes later, they were at The Friendly Bean. When they stepped out of the car, she could hardly contain her excitement. There was a beautiful patio. Within it stood an array of brown tables, each with its own glass center. On the left and right sides of the table, there stood two sky blue chairs to make the sets complete.

She looked at one set and decided to sit there, but not before Justin pulled up a chair for her before sitting down on his own. "So, you're probably wondering why I brought you here."

Maddie nodded.

"First, it's a treat for all of the hard work you've been doing, but it's also to help you learn how to express creativity in your baking. You're so used to following a cookbook that you're afraid to go outside the lines and do what *you* think is best for the cake."

Maddie squirmed in her seat, hating that he was right.

He put his hand on top of hers. "But I'm going to help you do that today," Justin called for the waiter to place their orders. "Now, after we've had lunch, pick what you want for dessert, okay?"

Maddie nodded, her eyes scanning the dessert menu. *The cheesecake looks good.*

She had a grilled chicken sandwich topped with fresh green lettuce, a slice of tomato, avocado, mayo, and a slice of pepper jack cheese while Justin had a burger topped with the same ingredients but with American cheese.

After they ate lunch, the waiter came back with the dessert. A decadent, rich cheesecake with raspberry sauce on top. Maddie looked at it with interest. "To be honest, this is my first-time trying cheesecake."

Justin blinked. "You've never tried it before."

She shook her head. "Never had a reason to."

Digging into the cheesecake, she took a small bite out of the decadent dessert. It tasted sweet, but not too sweet that it overpowered the raspberry sauce, which paired well with the dessert itself.

"This is really good. Thanks for bringing me here, Justin and planning the whole thing. That was very sweet of you."

Justin looked down at his shoes, trying to keep his gaze on her. "I'm glad you enjoyed it." He asked for the bill as Maddie began to bring out her purse. "Don't worry, I'll pay for it."

Maddie opened her mouth to speak, causing Justin to stop her. "I know you can pay for it yourself, but this is my treat to you. Just accept it, okay?"

She crossed her arms. "How about this? We can split the bill and both of us can be happy. It's not fair that you've been helping me all this time and not getting anything in return."

She heard a sigh escape from Justin's lips. "I'm helping you because I want to, Cupcake."

"Hmph!" *Okay, time to try another technique.* She waited until he looked up to give him a doe-eyed expression.

Justin grit his teeth in annoyance. "Oh, come on!"

She continued to give him the look until Justin finally caved.

"Okay, you've got yourself a deal," he relented.

Maddie stayed silent, getting a few twenties from her purse.

The drive back home was silent, as she noticed Justin was gripping the steering wheel hard but chose not to comment on. When they got back to her house, he scratched his ear.

"Everything okay?" she asked. She hoped she hadn't upset Justin or anything.

"Y–yeah. I just wanted to give you this." He walked back to his car and came with what looked to be a flower of some sort. The flower was a shade of party pink. It appeared in a spiral pattern, like the one you would find in a buttercup.

Maddie let out a small gasp before taking it from him, her heart fluttering at the kind gesture. "Thank you, Justin. It's beautiful, but... what is it?"

Justin shot her a teasing grin. "It's a pink ranunculus. As for what it means, I'll let you figure that one out."

Maddie stood there, hearing the hum of his car as he drove off. She heard her phone buzz in her pocket and looked to see a text. *Hope you enjoyed the cheesecake, Firecracker. Because that's exactly what we're going to be baking tomorrow. Get ready. :)*

She groaned. *What was this boy doing to her?*

Chapter 15

Sweet Victory

Friday, June 21, 2019

Maddie stifled a yawn, slowly getting up from her bed as she stretched her arms. The thought of baking with Justin got her excited, to the point where she felt giddy. *There go those butterflies again.*

She looked at the time on her clock. It read *8:30 a.m.* She groaned. Since she was up anyway, she figured she had better get a head start on her homework, which was due in a few days. *She knew she had to study for Tuesday's quiz; then she had to go to Justin's house for their baking lesson. What else was on her to-do list?*

She let out a sigh, feeling the hot water begin to cleanse her skin. *She had to feed her cat, Clara, get started on that school project that's due three weeks from now.* Turning off the water, she changed into something decent before running down the stairs.

Turning on her computer, she was eager to get the homework out of the way when she heard someone knock on the door.

Maddie rushed to the blinds, opening them to see Justin waving his hand towards her.

"You ready to get started?" he called out through the door.

"Yeah, just let me say bye to my family first," she replied.

Running up the stairs, she went to her parents' room, where her mom and dad were individually checking their phones. "See you, guys. Justin wants to teach me how to make cheesecake in the bakery."

Her dad looked up from his phone. He could be intimidating without meaning to. "Who's Justin?"

"R-r-remember?" Maddie stammered as she avoided looking him in the eyes. "He's one of my friends from college."

"Uh-huh. What's his social security number, and where does he live?"

"Dad... " she whined.

Her mom looked up from her phone, looking at her husband in the eyes. "Honey, he's a nice guy."

"He likes cats for Pete's sake. I've never met anyone at my workplace who likes evil," her dad muttered.

Maddie laughed. "You don't like anyone who likes cats, Dad."

He shook his head. "For good reason. Cats are evil."

She stifled a giggle that threatened to escape her lips. "Clara isn't evil. Remember, she tried to cuddle you once? She looked so sad when you rejected her."

"Good!" He muttered something incoherent, wondering how his family had become completely bewitched by the pest living in their garage.

Maddie rolled her eyes. "Anyway, I don't want to keep Justin waiting."

Her mother gave her a quick hug. "Bye, sweetie. Enjoy!"

Maddie waved goodbye to her parents, walking into her and her sister's room. "Hey, Mia. I'm off to bake with Justin."

Mia rubbed one of her eyes, still adjusting to the light in their room. "Don't you mean, your *crush*? she sang, a teasing glint in her eyes.

Maddie's skin grew warm at the mention of the topic. "Shut up, Mia," she snapped.

"Fine, I won't mention it again. Just be careful, okay? I don't want you crying again from a broken heart."

Maddie looked her in the eyes. "I won't, you can trust me on that," she said before she ran down the stairs and unlocked the door.

She came face to face with Justin's impeccable grin. "Good morning, Firecracker. Come on. We don't have time to waste."

"Hello to you, too, Justin. Did you sleep well?"

Justin turned his gaze towards her as they got inside the car. "Yeah, what about you?"

"A little. I'm a bit worried about the two quizzes I have this upcoming Tuesday."

He gave her a blank stare. "I thought you only had one quiz."

"I had a doctor's appointment on the day of my quiz, so the professor has decided to let me take the quiz I missed last week and the quiz for this coming week."

Justin looked at her in concern. "Is everything okay?"

Maddie looked out the window. "I'm okay. Just some health challenges but nothing I can't handle."

Justin stayed silent. "Not that I'm obligated to know, but why didn't you tell me?"

She shrugged. "I didn't want you to treat me any different."

He put a hand on her shoulder. "Why would I? That doesn't change the fact that you're the sweetest person I know. Just be sure to take it easy once in a while, okay?"

The brunette beamed at his concern for her well-being. "I will, thanks *Skyscraper*." She covered her mouth.

He fumed. "Hey, I'm not *that* tall!"

Maddie let out a snort. "Whatever you say."

"I'm not!"

Sure... "

"Let's just get going to the bakery," Justin said under his breath.

The drive was fast, as Maddie observed the drivers of the cars speed towards their destination, whether it be work or someplace else.

* * *

Twenty minutes later, they were at the bakery. When they got inside, Justin looked surprised to see all the ingredients for cheesecake were already laid out on the table in a neat row.

"Wow, Maddie. You came prepared."

Maddie sent a wink his way. "I learned from the best."

Justin directed his gaze from her to the fridge, his skin feeling warm at the sudden compliment.

His silence said it all as Maddie looked at him with a teasing grin. "Don't tell me you're getting flustered already, Valdez."

"Shut up... " he muttered, giving her a tiny smile.

They both walked up to the table, ready for what was in store for them.

"Okay, so I noticed that you put the Graham crackers in a Ziploc bag. That's perfect. So just smash them with a rolling pin a couple of times, and then roll it out until it's a fine texture," Justin instructed.

When Maddie was done, she mixed it in with the melted butter as she smoothed out the crust in a round eight-inch pan. Putting that in the fridge, Justin instructed her to mix the whipped cream, sugar, and lemon juice, along with the cream cheese in a separate bowl. Close to putting the cream cheese in, she stopped.

"What is it?" Justin asked.

"It feels like it needs a little something extra." She tapped her chin as she rummaged through the cabinets, desperate to find what she needed. "Ah, ha! Found it!" she exclaimed, reaching for the jar of honey, and putting a fourth of a cup into the mixture before adding the cream cheese and powdered gelatin mixture. "Just wanted to add a bit of flavor to the dessert."

His lips parted slightly. "You think honey will bring out the flavor more?"

She held eye contact with him. "I think it will turn out well. I have a good feeling about this."

He gave her hand a light squeeze. "Well, I'm excited to see how it turns out. No pressure."

Maddie reached for her phone, searching for the Spotify app. When she found the song she was looking for, she clicked on it, and *Little Bitty Pretty One* by Thurston Harris started playing from her phone.

Justin held back a laugh as he watched her dance and twirl around to the beat without a care in the world. Her laughter felt like music to his ears as he saw her in a whole new light. Her playful personality caused her to radiate the confidence she didn't know she had within her.

Walking back to the kitchen, Justin could see that she was glowing from head to toe.

Maddie turned to see him staring at her. "What?"

He grabbed her hand, placing a soft kiss on it. "Nothing. I like it when you smile and laugh. You should do that more often. It looks good on you."

Maddie stayed silent, his compliment causing her cheeks to redden. She poured the raspberries and sugar into a saucepan, watching the mixture began to thicken. When it was done, she added a little bit of mint for flavor before she brought the crust out from the fridge and strained the cream cheese mixture into the crust. Smoothing it out with a wooden spoon, she put it back in the fridge to set for an hour. "So, what do you want to do now?"

"You wanna watch Yumeiro pâtissier together?" Justin suggested.

"Maddie gave him a quick nod. "You know I'm not going to say no to that."

As they watched the show on his phone, time seemed to pass by and, before they knew it, the cake was ready to be eaten. Maddie grabbed a pie slicer from the drawer closest to her, grabbing forks for the two of them.

"This is delicious, Cupcake. Adding honey was a nice touch," Justin took another bite of his slice.

Maddie stuttered out a response. "I-i-it's no big deal. I just went with what I thought would make the dessert taste better."

"Well, you have the stamp of approval."

"By whom, if I may ask?"

"Me, of course."

As the two friends enjoyed their dessert, Maddie couldn't help but feel like things were changing between them and the worst part about it? She couldn't stop herself from falling.

Chapter 16

A Friend in Need

Saturday, June 22, 2019

Maddie's face twisted into a grimace at the thought of how she had tried to juggle both work and summer classes.

* * *

*On the summer of **July 11, 2017**, she had decided to work as a waitress at a local restaurant. The place was famous for its food as well as its friendly atmosphere. Within a few months of starting the job, she was beginning to get the hang of things. Things were new to her, from serving food to the customers to replacing the coffee to wiping down the tables when they left. She walked around the room, picking up the apron from the stand and tying it around her waist.*

The sweet smell of hot chocolate filled the air. Maddie just stood and took it all in for a moment. The restaurant had a quaint sort of look to it, pictures varying in color and size on a separate wall close to the kitchen. She snapped out of her reverie, hearing the bell on the door chime.

"Maddie?"

She turned around to see the stranger, feeling her cheeks flush when she recognized who it was. Even in casual clothing, she knew style when she saw it. Justin was dressed in a blue t-shirt and white shorts, wiping the sweat off his forehead with his hand.

"Order up!" Her gaze turned from him to the food she needed to serve.

She sent an apologetic glance Justin's way, a bit frustrated they couldn't talk more. They gazed at each other for what seemed like hours before Maddie broke it and started to scold herself. Her eyes scanned the information of the ticket, her eyes darting back and forth to read it. She touched the back of the plates with her fingers, making sure they weren't too hot.

Quickly but carefully, she picked up the plates, making sure she got to the right table. "Here you go!" She called out to the table, making sure she got each customer's request correct, bringing the plates down with grace. A squeal distracted her, causing Maddie to made eye contact with a baby. His brown hair, blue eyes, and chubby cheeks made him look even cuter than before.

"Aw, hi!" Maddie said, playing peek-a-boo with him.

The baby laughed, causing Maddie to laugh in spite of herself. It wasn't until someone cleared their throat behind her that she felt shivers go down her spine. She turned around to see her boss with a warm expression on her face.

"Maddie... " her boss started softly.

She gave a curtsy to her boss. "Sorry Miss Ingrid, I'll get back to work." Scurrying back to the kitchen, she took orders and walked from table to table, making sure she didn't bump into anyone.

An hour later, she felt that someone was watching her but didn't know who. She sang the familiar tune of The Cup Song, feeling her mood grow brighter with every note. When she finished, the two bystanders closest to her politely clapped, having enjoyed the free entertainment.

Maddie gave them a small smile, taking a bow before letting her boss know that she was leaving.

"Hey, wait up!" someone called out. She turned to see Justin running up toward her.

He ran a hand through his hair. "You were awesome out there. I just... you know... wanted you to know that."

She felt her breath hitch at the compliment but tried to play it cool by dismissing it. "Thanks!"

An awkward silence was felt between the two before she spoke up.

"Well, see you later, pal!" She gave him a playful punch to the arm.

"See you later, Firecracker!" Justin tried to retract his words. "Cupcake! I meant Maddie. See ya!"

Maddie felt Amber's presence loom over her as she walked up behind her with an amused expression on her face. She gritted her teeth. "Not a word, Amber. Not a single word!"

The two friends walked side by side when Maddie stopped when she got an alert on her phone. As she typed on her phone, she froze. Fear crippled her heart as she looked at the grade in shame. She hadn't been doing so well on her Spanish tests and this was the third D she received.

Amber's hand on her shoulder brought her back to reality. "You okay, Mads?" she asked, looking at her with a frown.

Maddie quickly put on a small smile, not wanting to worry her. "Yeah, I'm good. I just need to talk to my professor about something."

The two were silent, with Maddie trying to comprehend the information she had just received. All of her tests were worth sixty-five percent of her grade if she remembered correctly. It was looking more likely that she would have to take the class again.

"Hey." She looked up at the figure in question, pleased to see that it was Justin and not some stranger.

A sad sigh escaped her lips. "Hey."

The three friends were silent as Maddie felt her friends' curiosity grow.

Justin motioned for her to get on to his back. "I know something's upset you and I know piggyback rides make you feel better. So, hop on. Maybe when we get to your house, we can talk about what's bothering you."

She smiled as the trio walked towards her house, with the brunette thankful that her parents weren't back from their trip to movies yet. She wasn't sure she could handle the onslaught of questions they would have right now.

Amber tapped on the door, while Maddie slid off Justin's back, thanking him for the piggyback ride.

Mia opened the door, her mouth agape when she saw Maddie and her friends were back so early. "Hey, you guys, what's–" She took a look at Maddie's face. "What happened? Did someone hurt you?"

Maddie let out a small laugh, thankful for her sister's sense of humor. The trio came inside the house, as Mia locked the door behind them. "No, no one hurt me. Just another failed test."

"Hmmm, have you tried tutoring?" Mia suggested.

It was then that Maddie, for some unknown reason, felt a surge of anger rise up from within her. "For your information, I have, and it didn't work," she snapped. She took a deep breath. "I'm sorry. I just... hoped that I would have done better on the next test. Spanish isn't really my strong suit." She glided her foot across the rug, silence accompanying her words.

"That doesn't mean you won't do better on the next test. Ask your professor for pointers if you have to," Justin encouraged.

Maddie nodded her head as she, Amber, Justin and Mia began to brainstorm on ways to study.

Soon after, Miss Ingrid walked over to her while she was cleaning the tables. "Listen, Maddie. As much as I love having you around here, I don't want your education to suffer because of it. I know you told me about your last test grade, so why don't we have you take some time off, and you could come back and work during the holidays, sounds good?"

Maddie nodded, her heart feeling a little lighter as she walked away from her boss.

* * *

Looking back now, Maddie smiled to herself as her mind mulled over the events that had occurred that day, feeling thankful that she had an awesome sister and even better friends.

Chapter 17

Old Feelings

Tuesday, June 25, 2019

Maddie trudged her feet along the wooden floor of the library, her legs aching as she gave her college ID to the young security guard, who proceeded to let her in. She looked up to see Justin, who waved at her as she passed by. Hoping she would feel better, she walked over to him, butterflies in her stomach. She could feel herself looking over her outfit once more. *Did she have something stuck in her teeth? That would be so embarrassing!*

"Wow, you look terrible!" he teased.

Charlotte stood beside him, looking shocked at how blunt Justin was. She slapped his arm. "You don't just say things like that to a girl."

Maddie waved nonchalantly. "Don't worry about it. I know he's only teasing."

Charlotte shook her head. "Figures. His mouth is bigger than his head, anyways."

Maddie snickered.

"Hey!" Justin shouted, offended at the accusation. He turned to Maddie. "Maddie, can you please tell her to knock it off?"

She shook her head, still giggling at Charlotte's sly comment.

"Thanks for making me laugh, you guys. I needed it."

Charlotte raised an eyebrow. "What's gotten you upset?"

Maddie sighed. "I'm a bit nervous at how my group presentation went. On the bright side, one of my team members acknowledged the work I did, saying that he appreciated how, despite being nervous, decided to use that energy towards making sure everything went smoothly."

Justin tapped his chin. "I remember you told me about that. Don't beat yourself up over it. I can tell you're the type of person that would do well on the project."

She turned her head away, hoping he wouldn't see the blush on her cheeks. "Well, thank you."

Charlotte nodded. "I agree with Justin. You're probably the type who bites more than she can chew, right?"

Maddie nodded, slumping her shoulders.

She quickly picked up on Maddie's mood change. "Hey, don't worry about it." She slapped a hand on Justin's shoulder. "You don't know how many times I've had to tell this guy here the same thing."

Justin crossed his arms. "I'm right here."

Maddie laughed, her eyes sparkling with mischief. *She's probably where he gets the rest of his personality from.*

Charlotte snickered. "Anyway, I'm sure you did well on the project. I mean, I understand if you were nervous about people staring at you and everything, but you probably did *way* better than you think you did."

Justin tapped his chin. "I'm sure you did well. I'm guessing you're the person who delegated roles to each member of the group."

Maddie cleared her throat. "I am." She opened her mouth, then closed it, unsure of what to say. She then slightly turned her gaze away from her friends.

He looked at Maddie, noticing the way she clenched and unclenched her fingers. "Everything okay, Maddie?"

She took in a deep breath, trying to get herself to relax. "Yeah, I'm just thinking. I've made a couple of friends that seem really cool. Plus, some of them are from my former classes."

Charlotte lit up. "That's amazing!"

Maddie gave her a small smile. "You're one of those people, you know."

Charlotte looked taken aback, taking the compliment in stride. "Oh... well... You aren't so bad, yourself. Justin's shown me a couple of your drawings. They're really cool. Wish I could learn to draw like that."

Maddie diverted her gaze away, her cheeks growing pink.

Charlotte continued. "And before you ask, *yes*, that's a compliment."

"Thanks for the pep talk, guys. I feel much better now." Maddie pulled out her phone from her pocket, wanting to see what grade she and her team members got for their presentation.

"What are you doing?" Charlotte's eyes widened, having a feeling of what her friend was about to do.

Maddie hid her phone from their view. "Nothing, just checking to see if my professor updated the grade on our school website."

"Maddie." Justin stepped toward her, walking toward her. "Get away from the phone."

"No." She ran as fast as her legs could carry her to the elevator. "Not if you can catch me first."

Justin looked toward the elevator, then Charlotte, then back to the elevator.

"Well, what are you waiting for? Go get her, tiger!" Maddie heard Charlotte say, ushering him toward the elevator, waving goodbye to him as its doors started to close.

She watched as Justin sprinted towards the elevator, putting his hand in between the doors. "Not so tough now, huh Firecracker?" He swiped the phone away from her, causing her to gasp.

"Hey, give it back!"

"No way, this phone is mine now."

Maddie continued to reach for the prized possession, stretching as high as her arm would allow her to. She jumped up and down, her annoyance increasing as Justin held it up even higher. *It was times like these where she wished she were taller.*

"I said give it—"

She tripped over his shoe or *would* have if Justin hadn't caught her.

"Woah, you okay?"

He held her by the arms, looking her in the eye with concern.

"Yeah, I'm—"

The words died down on her lips, feeling a lump in her throat. Her gaze lingered on him for a few seconds longer before the feelings she once had for him started to resurface.

All the cherished memories that happened between them came hurtling toward her as they merged themselves into one massive clump. It all became too much for her to bear as she ran out of the elevator.

Maddie ignored the sound of Justin calling out for her as she pushed open the door that led to the girls' bathroom, locking the door of one of the empty stalls.

Maddie's heart thumped in her chest as she tried to calm herself down. She couldn't deny it any longer. She was beginning to have feelings for Justin all over again. Now she had to answer the question of where they should go from here.

Chapter 18

Good Intentions

Thursday, June 27, 2019

Mia sat across from Maddie, leaning back in an armchair while steepling her fingers. "So, you have feelings for Justin."

"We went over that already," Maddie mumbled into her pillow.

"So, you've had feelings for this guy for five years... " Mia said, ignoring the way her older sister groaned into her pillow. "You feel like he likes you and you like him." She twiddled with her pen, twirling in a way that seemed extra. "Frankly, I don't see what the problem is."

Maddie slowly got up from lying down on her bed, being careful not to twist anything. "I just don't want to get hurt again, that's all." She tightly hugged her pillow, wishing the whirlwind of emotions she was feeling right now would go away.

"Maddie," Maddie looked up from the pillow towards Mia, who gave her a small smile. "I know Justin, and he isn't the type of guy to do things out of the blue. He probably had a good reason for letting you down gently."

She winced. "I know. He told me he didn't know how he felt about me yet."

"Maybe he has feelings for you, and you just don't know it yet?" Mia questioned.

Maddie shrugged. "Maybe."

The two sisters were silent for a moment, that is, until Mia heard some commotion coming from downstairs. "I'll be right back." She ran down the stairs, stopping when she saw her dad and Justin talking for a moment.

"Sir, I like Maddie a lot," she heard Justin declare.

Mia blinked. She watched the scene play out before her, noticing the way Justin slightly rocked himself back and forth with his feet. Time stood still as her dad looked at the boy with a hard glare. She would not want to be him right now.

Her dad let out a grunt of disapproval. "And how can I make sure you won't hurt my daughter again?"

Mia winced. Her dad made a good point.

Justin chewed on his bottom lip, trying to figure out what to say next.

"I didn't know how I felt about your daughter yet, and now I do." Mia watched as he held his head high. He cleared his throat. "I want to ask your daughter out on a date. I promise it will be in a public setting, and you guys can come as well if you need extra proof."

He licked his lips. "She's funny, smart, and has a great personality, but the most beautiful thing about her is her willingness to put others' needs before her own."

Her dad chuckled. "That's funny because that's one of the things I taught her when she was growing up."

Justin smiled. "As you know, I went to culinary school for two years and decided to go back to college to complete my bachelor's degree in rhetoric and composition. I'm planning on using both of those degrees to good use: one to become a pastry chef and the other to become an editor for a literary magazine." He looked her dad in the eye. "While I can't be sure I won't hurt her feelings, I can promise I'll treat her with the utmost respect that she deserves, yet give her room to be human."

Silence passed between the two of them before Maddie's dad gave Justin a soft smile. "You have my blessing. I'm choosing to trust that you'll treat her well. But if you break her heart again... " He put a hand on Justin's shoulders, giving him a tight smile. "I'll tear you from limb to limb. Understand?"

Justin rapidly nodded his head, afraid of what would happen if he decided to speak.

"You have mine as well." Maddie and Mia's mother called out from the living room, doing some work on her laptop. "I heard the whole conversation, and I approve. Just one *tiny* detail." Their mother tightly grabbed Justin's shoulder, making sure to get her message across. "If you hurt my daughter again, there *will* be hell to pay. While I understand that you weren't obligated to accept my daughter's feelings, the pain that she felt that day would be *nothing* compared to the pain you'll feel if you mess this up. Am I clear?"

Justin shrunk back, fearing what would happen if he moved. "Crystal."

"Oh, and one more thing," their mom added.

"What?" Justin asked, a feeling of dread washing over him.

Maddie's mother pointed to where Mia was standing. *Shit!* Mia slowly came out from her hiding spot, crossing her arms. "You didn't even ask my opinion, Justin. But for the record, you have my approval as well."

"Please don't tell Maddie yet." Justin pleaded, putting his hands together.

"You're lucky I closed the door to me and Maddie's bedroom, or she would have heard *everything.*

Justin gulped. "Well, it was nice seeing you guys. Tell Maddie I said that I wanted to talk to her, bye!" He quickly rushed out the door, slamming it from behind.

"Such a nice boy," their mom commented.

"Shame, he left so quickly," Mia responded as the two ladies shared a laugh.

Chapter 19

Girls' Day Out

Saturday, June 29, 2019

Maddie walked alongside Mia, Charlotte, and Amber as the sun's rays started to warm her skin. Earlier that day, Charlotte had told them that she finally posted her art onto Tumblr and was excited the second she clicked *post,* so they decided to celebrate that. The group of friends walked along the sidewalk, chit-chatting about the exciting news.

Maddie gave her a pat on the back. "That's amazing! I'm so proud of you!"

She looked away, bashful. "It's just a little something I've been working on for the past few weeks. It's not like I'm the next Pablo Picasso or anything."

"You don't give yourself enough credit!" Amber piped up, determined to bring up her friend's confidence.

Maddie struggled to catch up with the trio, her mind wandering as the thought of her next assignment came to mind. The trio looked back at her as they waited for her to catch up with them.

Charlotte was the one who spoke up first. "What's up?"

Maddie stopped in her tracks as she sucked in a deep breath. "I'm just a bit worried about how the rest of my summer classes will go."

Charlotte blinked. "I thought you said you got an A+ on that assignment."

Maddie let out a huff, blowing a strand of her hair out of her eyes. "I did... only to find out that I failed one of the quizzes we had last week."

"Ouch... " Amber commented.

"Yeah, so I decided to go to my professor during his office hours and see how I can bump up my grade or at least get an A on the next quiz."

"Sounds like a game plan!" Charlotte exclaimed.

Maddie nodded as the four went to the mall to take some time away from their classes. It was a sweltering, hot afternoon as she breathed a sigh of contentment. The hustle and bustle of the building provided a stark contrast from how quiet it was outside. People walked from store to store, trying on cute outfits as she saw one girl try on a hat with a little, cute bow on the side of it.

The place felt so cramped that she and the others had to swerve left and right as they tried not to bump into people.

"You okay, sis?" Mia asked, looking towards her sister as she rubbed her back.

"Yeah, it's just a little bit crowded. Nothing I can't handle, though."

The four of them walked into various stores as they each looked at arrays of cute outfits that hung on the racks. A lovely top caught Maddie's eye. It had a blue and white striped pattern, like a sailor's outfit. *This top looks like it would be my style.* She took the top from the rack, turning over the price tag. She did a double-take. *Fifty bucks?* She let out a disappointed sigh as she put the top back on the rack, upset that it wasn't within her budget.

Maddie and her friends walked around the mall as they looked inside different stores. After they got tired of walking from shop to shop, they walked into a nice restaurant to get something to eat. The waiter sat them down, giving them menus before coming back with water to drink.

"So, what's the deal with you and Justin?" Amber inquired as Maddie began to sip a glass of water. When hearing Amber's question, Maddie choked on it, with Mia rubbing her back.

Charlotte turned to look at Amber. "Damn, girl... you don't hold back, do you?"

"We were all thinking it, so why postpone the inevitable?" Amber responded bluntly.

"Nothing... I sort of left him hanging," Maddie said in a rushed tone.

"Wait, what? You *left* Justin hanging? The boy you've had a crush on for eight freaking years?"

"Way to go, Amber," Mia muttered under her breath.

"Sorry, it's just... you guys need to talk this out... for both your sake. Otherwise, you guys will end up right back where you started."

Maddie knew Amber was right. As she dug into her food, a question laid on her mind. *Was it worth the risk?* As they ate their meals in silence, her phone began to ring. She sent an apologetic glance to her friends. "Sorry you guys, but I have to take this. It's Miss Caroline calling. I'll be just a few minutes."

Maddie raced outside the restaurant, not wanting to disturb the people who were having a nice, quiet meal with their loved ones. "Hey, Miss Caroline. What can I do for you?"

"Hello, darling. Nice to hear from you again. Sorry to bother you on your day off, but it turns out I need more help than I realized I would."

"What do you mean?" Maddie asked slowly, her stomach churning with unease.

"Well... " Miss Caroline looked back at the baker who threw her hat down in anger and marched right out of the building she was in. "The person I asked to make all of the desserts for my wedding just quit, so I may have told my guests that you would step up to the plate."

"What?" Maddie shrieked, causing some onlookers to look at her weirdly. "But I thought I was only supposed to work on the wedding cake... " she stated, feeling her palms begin to sweat.

"Well, you *are* a baker, right?" Miss Caroline questioned in a condescending tone.

"Y-y-y-yes I am, but... " Maddie stuttered, not liking the direction this conversation was going.

"And you *did* promise that you would make my wedding cake for me, correct?"

Maddie found herself sweating bullets. "Yes, but I... "

"So, this shouldn't be a problem for you since you're used to baking all the time."

Maddie let out a reluctant sigh. "Yes, Miss Caroline."

"Wonderful. I'll see you then," Miss Caroline said in her usual cheery tone.

As she ended the call, Maddie felt her blood pressure begin to rise once more. *Who does she think she is, treating me like that?* she fumed, trying to remain as unaffected by the situation as possible. She walked back into the restaurant, putting on a fake smile while dusting her dress off.

Mia tilted her head sideways. She knew something had gone wrong by the way her eyes flashed with rage. "Maddie, I hate to ask, but is everything–"

"Yep, everything is fine," Maddie interrupted, her response sounding an octave higher than her usual tone.

"Really?" Charlotte asked, looking doubtful. "Your right eye is twitching."

Damn it! Maddie cursed, wishing she hadn't inherited that bad habit from her mom. She relayed the story to her friends. Afterward, she found Amber gripping the table for dear life. "If you want my opinion, Miss Caroline is acting like a real b–"

Mia quickly covered Amber's mouth, silencing her with a glare.

Amber turned towards her. "What's the difference when you curse, huh?"

"Mine isn't intentional," Mia shot back with gritted teeth.

Amber took a glance at Mia's expression. "I'm sure your innocent older sister has heard *far* worse, Mia. You guys go to the same college. She's bound to hear people swear once in a while and you've even admitted to letting one slip every once in a while."

Charlotte rolled her eyes at their behavior. "*Anyway,* have you figured out what you're going to do?"

"I'm going to ask Justin if he can come over to my house and help me make the other desserts." Maddie winced. "If he isn't too mad at me for leaving him at the library."

"Are you kidding? He knows you didn't mean it. I'm sure you guys will be fine," Amber piped up.

"Not with all that sexual tension brewing," Charlotte muttered as she sipped her glass of water.

Maddie laughed nervously, unsure of whether Charlotte was right. *There was no denying it. She was screwed.*

Chapter 20

A Breath of Fresh Air

Tuesday, July 2, 2019

Justin gripped the steering wheel, trying to keep his emotions in check as he recalled the voicemail Firecracker had left on his phone. *Hey Justin. I'm in a bit of jam and desperately need your help. Not that you have anything to worry about, of course. Everything's fine over here.*

Cars honked to and fro as he kept his eyes on the road. Questions lingered in his mind. *Is Firecracker okay? Did something happen?* Whatever the case was, he knew her voice sounded shaky on the phone. Justin pulled into the driveway of her house, knocking on the door with a sense of urgency.

Maddie's mom greeted him, looking just as surprised as he was. "Justin? What are you doing here?"

Justin cleared his throat. "Hi, Miss Jones. Good to see you. I just wanted to see how Maddie's holding up."

Her mom's eyes flitted around the room, avoiding his gaze. "Honestly, she told me about the situation, and while I am proud of her for stepping up to the challenge, I'm also angry."

Justin tilted his head. "Why? Is she hurt or anything?"

Her mom paused. "Physically? Yes. Emotionally? It's hard to say. It's better if you see for yourself."

Her mother led Justin to the kitchen, where Mia was rubbing Maddie's shoulder, in hopes of providing some comfort. Maddie quickly wiped her eyes. "Oh, hey, Justin. I didn't hear you come in."

Justin gave her a tight smile as he pulled up a chair to sit down beside her. He quickly hugged her. Shock registered in Maddie's face before she slowly reciprocated the hug, wrapping her arms around his shoulder. Her mom and Mia looked at one another knowingly as they spoke in hushed tones. The two let go of each other, feeling awkward as soon as the tender moment was over.

Maddie relayed the story play by play, noticing how Justin clenched his jaws, getting more livid with every sentence she told him. She paused, waiting for him to respond.

"I should have known my aunt would pull something like this. She never thinks that the person who's doing the work has feelings as well," Justin remarked, rubbing his forehead. "Well, there's no backing out of it since you already agreed to it," he started, with Maddie having the decency to look ashamed at her actions.

Maddie paced back and forth, trying to come up with a plan. "What if we each devote a day to making each pastry once you get the invoice from her and raise the price since I'm doing more work than we agreed on?"

"I like the sound of that, but I'm afraid my aunt won't like the sound of that," Justin said, thinking of the furious look on his aunt's face once he told her the news. He shuddered. "But I'll be behind you every step of the way." He pulled her in for another hug, but wasn't prepared for her to bury her face into his chest. He looked down at her, feeling his face turn scarlet at how close she was to him.

"I think my sister has taken a liking to you," Mia piped up.

"I think so too," Her mom added, laughing at the way her eldest daughter held on tightly to him.

Maddie looked around her for a moment, suddenly remembering where she was. She dusted herself off, clearing her throat. "Sorry," she mumbled.

Justin kissed the top of her forehead. "No problem, Cupcake. A little warning next time though." He watched as Maddie turned her gaze toward her mother, who had a playful grin on her face. "Me and your sister are here if you need any help."

"You guys... " Maddie said, feeling overwhelmed by how much her family and Justin were willing to help her.

"I already called Charlotte and Amber, and they've agreed to help," Mia said, scribbling who was responsible for what pastry on a sheet of paper.

Justin laid a hand on Maddie's shoulder. "We'll let you take the lead on things, of course. I want you to learn that you can do this if you put your mind to it... "

"I heard the whole conversation from over here. Just let me know how I can help," her dad echoed from across the living room.

"Can Clara help... you know, by tasting the desserts?" Justin heard Maddie ask her dad, walking over to the living room to give him a pleading look.

Justin had to stifle a chuckle when he heard his response as he imagined the expressionless look on her dad's face when he looked up from his work. "No!"

Mia pouted while Justin laughed at the banter between Maddie and her dad.

In the kitchen, Justin admired Maddie from afar, seeing her in a whole new way. He shook his head. She never ceased to amaze him. Now he knew what he was missing a few years ago when they were sixteen.

She was a bright, refreshing light in a world tainted by darkness. Even though he rejected her, his feelings for her never waned. He believed John Keats said it best when he said, "I am profoundly enchanted by the flowing complexity in you."

He leaned against the wall with his arms crossed, watching Maddie laugh with her family.

"Well, I gotta get going. I'll see you later, okay?" He gave her a playful punch to the arm. "See ya next Wednesday."

Turning the doorknob, he stopped when he heard Maddie run up to him. "Wait." She gasped, catching a breath. "I just realized that I hadn't met your parents before since you took me out to eat so... " She spun her index fingers around each other in a circular motion. "Do you mind if I tag along with you to meet them?"

Justin smiled. "Sure, as long as it's okay with your family."

Maddie's parents looked at each other knowingly. "Go ahead, sweetie. Have fun."

"But not too much fun," Mia added.

Maddie waved goodbye to them, with Justin locking the door behind them. With their seatbelts buckled, he pulled out of the driveway and onto the road. A few minutes later, they got to his house. Maddie knocked on the door with a shaky breath, her nerves getting the better of her.

"Don't worry about a thing. My parents already know you and everything. You've got this." His words of confidence had its desired effect on her, feeling her shaking come to a steady halt.

Justin rang the doorbell, booping Maddie's nose and smiling when she gave him a genuine laugh. "You should laugh more often. It looks good on you."

He heard her gasp, lightly punching his shoulder whenever she got annoyed or embarrassed.

The door opened to reveal a tall, confident woman. She stood before her son, looking down at the girl he brought along with him. Her voluminous, wavy brown hair reached past her shoulders, complimenting her beige complexion.

His mother's eyes squinted in recognition as she recognized the girl who was her son's best friend. "Hola querida. How have you been?" she greeted in a thick accent that caused Maddie to hang on to every word.

She looked Justin's mom in the eye. *Well, here goes nothing.* "He estado muy bien. Gracias. And yourself?"

Justin's mom looked pleased with Maddie. "Elegiste uno bueno, muchacho. I wouldn't be surprised if your dad ended up approving of her as well."

Maddie beamed with pride, thankful for the few Spanish classes she took during her spring semester, and Google Translate, of course. Ever since she learned that Justin and his family spoke Spanish, she tried her hardest to learn the language so that she could understand them. Justin had done so much for her in the past few weeks. It was the least she could do, plus she got to know him a bit more.

"Honey, come here. Justin's little friend is at the door," his mom yelled out.

"Mama, please... " Justin pleaded, hoping his parents wouldn't embarrass him to the point where he would have to move schools.

A tall, lean man walked towards the door, his skin a deep brown. His glasses weren't your average everyday "thick frames." Instead, they were a semi-rimmed shape in an intimidating shade of velvet black. His beard matched the color of his glasses, trailing along the sides of his face, completely covering his chin. His hair was what men would describe as a temple fade with sponge twists at the top.

He smiled, shaking Maddie's hand. "It's a pleasure to see you again, Miss Jones. Our son over here has told us so much about you." His voice was deep but calming, his tone making Maddie chuckle.

Justin's face paled.

"He has?" Maddie asked, looking back at Justin with a grin.

"Oh, *yes*. You wouldn't believe how much time Justin spends yapping on and on about the girl of his dreams–"

"Okay!" Justin came up from behind Maddie, pushing her towards his car. "I think it's time we said our goodbyes now."

Justin's father let out a hearty laugh. "Okay, love you, son."

Justin muttered to himself, pushing Maddie faster and faster towards the passenger's seat.

"You're not going to say it back?"

Justin looked over to his dad, who sported a cheeky grin. He pinched the bridge of his nose, looking back to see him holding a megaphone to his mouth. *He wouldn't...* His eyes darted from left to right, sweating bullets when he saw his neighbors coming out to see what all the fuss was about. "Dad, please stop," he pleaded once more.

"Tell me you love me. Then this will all be over," Justin's dad spoke into the megaphone.

He would. He definitely would. Justin looked up toward the sky, praying that this embarrassing moment would end soon. He looked at his neighbors' children, some of them giggling at the situation before them. *They were probably gonna talk about this for weeks on end.*

"Love you too, Dad," Justin said with a reluctant tone.

His dad grinned. "That's what I'd like to hear. Now, Maddie, would you like to see some cute pictures of Justin when he was young? I promise that you won't be disappointed."

Justin ushered Maddie towards the car door at lightning speed before she could reply. "Move, woman, move!" he prompted, shutting the car doors after him, and driving off.

Maddie burst out laughing at Justin's antics, looking from behind him to see his parents waving to the two of them. She waved back before Justin eased his foot on the car's pedal.

Chapter 21

Pushing Forward

Friday, July 5, 2019

Maddie looked at the group of friends and family members by her side, ready to get work. She held the whisk in her hand like a drill sergeant would with his soldiers. "Okay, everyone, we have exactly *twelve* days to get everything ready. I know it's a lot of work, but I believe that we can do it. Now, who's with me?" she finished, her head held high.

Everyone cheered at her motivational speech.

"Mom, you and Dad can make the brownies."

"Yes, ma'am," she said, getting to work with her husband as they compiled the list of ingredients.

"Charlotte, you and Amber can compile the list of ingredients for the red velvet cupcakes," Maddie instructed.

"On it, Captain."

"And before you ask, *no*, you cannot eat one," Maddie said before giving Amber a pointed look.

Amber looked deflated. "Aww... " she said, making the others laugh.

"Justin and I will work on getting all the ingredients for the desserts at the grocery store and the cake decorations at the flower store today," Maddie said before she and Justin walked towards the door.

"No funny business," Maddie's dad called out.

"Dad, please... " Maddie groaned, feeling her cheeks turn pink as Justin laughed.

Justin shut the door behind them as they closed the door to his car. "I have the utmost faith in you that we'll be able to do this," he said, putting his hand upon Maddie's.

Her eyes sparkled with excitement. "Thanks, Justin. That means a lot to me."

He nodded as he reversed out of the driveway and onto the road. While he drove, Maddie looked out the window. The sun had peeked out from behind the clouds, with children riding on their bicycles in the warm weather. She rested her chin in the palm of her hand, looking as adorable as ever. While she was enjoying the scenery, her mind went racing with a game plan on how to get things done. *Let's see. They needed to head to the grocery store to pick up the ingredients for the cake. After that, they needed to go to the flower store to pick up the flowers for the cake topper. On Wednesday, they would go to his house to get things started. Maddie*

*will take care of the cake while he stood
close by in case she needed any help.*

As Maddie went over her mental to-do
list, she felt Justin was looking at her. She
looked back at him, causing him to turn his
gaze toward the road in front of him,
whistling innocently. "What, what is it?"

Justin felt a bead of sweat run down his
forehead. "Oh, it's nothing."

Maddie narrowed her eyes at him.
"Weren't you staring at me just now?"

He gulped, pulling the collar of his t-shirt.
"Hey, isn't this your favorite song?" He
turned the volume of the radio up to distract
her, wincing when he realized he turned it up
too loud.

"Justin, turn it down!" Maddie screamed,
covering her ears at its intensity.

"Oops, sorry!" He turned the volume
down, causing her to remove her hands from
her ears.

"What's gotten into you?" she chastised.

He shrugged, mentally beating himself
up.

Maddie put a hand on his shoulder,
rubbing it. "It's okay. I know you didn't mean
it."

He sighed, pulling into the store's parking
lot. "Thanks. You ready to go?"

They both shut their respective sides of the car behind them as they walked inside. The store was huge. Long aisles lined up against one another, with the name of various sections and what was in each aisle written in bold. People ran to and fro, getting what they needed to make the meals for that week. A kid who looked five years old pointed to a treat he wanted to buy while his mother pulled him in the opposite direction, causing him to whine in protest.

"Let's do this," Maddie said, grabbing a shopping cart.

Justin nodded as he heard a *ding* come from his phone. He reached into his back pocket, quickly reading the text. *Hey Justin. It's Charlotte. Here is the list of ingredients we need you to get from the store to start baking this week.* He went through the list in its entirety, looking surprised when he noticed chili powder in the ingredients for brownies, which he immediately brought to Maddie's attention.

She looked at the list, rubbing her neck when she noticed the extra ingredient. "I thought the brownies could use a little 'kick' to them."

"You're the boss, Mads."

The two strolled into the *dairy* section, with Justin picking up unsalted butter, buttermilk, three cartons of free-range eggs, heavy cream, plus cream cheese, and putting the items into the cart. The two walked into the baking section as Maddie began to look for the brand of chocolate chips she was looking for.

She turned to Justin to speak for a minute. "You have couverture chocolate at home, right?"

Justin chuckled. "You underestimate me, Cupcake. A baker is always ready for the unexpected."

Maddie used her hand to conceal her laugh. "Glad to know I can always count on you, Skyscraper."

Once she found the brand she was looking for, the pair quickly went up to the line full of people ready to purchase their items. They lined up, Justin patiently waiting while Maddie did the exact opposite. Justin turned to the side, noticing Maddie fiddling with her phone.

"You okay?" he asked.

"Yeah, just crossing out the items to make sure we got everything on the list," Maddie quickly looked at the group text, compiled of her family's and her friends' phone numbers. She checked off the items one by one, feeling a sense of accomplishment as each of the items were crossed out.

The cashier quickly scanned the items, giving the pair a quick, but friendly greeting as a grocer bagged each of the items and put them in the cart. Once the two were done, they were off to the crafts' store, where they looked for cake decorations, along with other things that they needed.

"Do you have all the necessary things we'll need to carry the cake by any chance?" Justin asked, filling the cart with necessary items, noticing a pack of paper plates with a simple, beautiful design.

"Yeah, I'm just a bit nervous about how everything will turn out," Maddie confided, reaching between the top and bottom shelves to get a pack of forks, knives, and spoons for four dollars. No need to buy something expensive. She knew Justin's aunt had an expensive taste, but that didn't mean that she had to break her bank account to please her.

Justin stopped in his tracks, turning to look Maddie in the eye. "I know my aunt can be a bit much sometimes, but you're not alone. You've got us to help you."

Maddie gave him a genuine smile. "I know, and I'm lucky to have all of you actually, not just you. I mean, I'm confident enough to know I can get the job done, I just doubt myself sometimes," she rambled on.

He put a hand on her cheek, easing her nervousness. "I get it, Firecracker, but I believe I'm the lucky one," he whispered, rendering her speechless.

Walking towards the cashier, he waited for her to catch up while she just stood there, unable to move. Maddie gingerly touched her cheek, feeling like she was thirteen all over again. It was good to know that she could count on him, as well as her family and friends, whenever she started to doubt herself. She smiled, letting that thought settle in her mind. She caught up to where Justin was, ready to see this project to the finish.

Chapter 22

Two Hearts, One Love

Saturday, July 13, 2019

It was a summer wedding in the late afternoon. Everything was set up to the bride's expectations, or at least, Maddie had hoped so. Everyone had pitched in to help, from setting up the table to bringing the desserts in from the backseat of the car. Red velvet cupcakes topped with decadent cream cheese frosting were lined up on a rustic, golden cupcake tray. The brownies and chocolate chip cookies were lined up against one another with a neat row, which were covered in a clear, plastic cover. The last of them all was the truffle cake. She and Justin had outdone themselves, given that it was the first time she made this sort of thing. The chocolate cake was made with a rich, truffle filling. A stunning floral centerpiece made up of Hanoi ranunculus flowers and white gardenias sat on top of the cake. Maddie had wanted to add her own touch on the centerpiece, so she had decided that those flowers were the best complement to Miss Caroline's wedding cake.

Maddie took a deep breath as the flower girl walked down the aisle. *She looks so cute in her white dress.* The little girl threw flowers onto the ground, bringing smiles to everyone's faces. The next people to come were the bridesmaids, every one of them dressed in satin, purple gowns. The groomsmen came next, with Justin in tow. He gave a wink to Maddie, who turned her gaze away. He imagined that her face would be crimson right about now. Afterward, the groom arrived with his mother, with her wrapping her arm around his. Trailing down the aisle, they stopped once they were in front of the groomsmen and bridesmaids. At last, everyone arose from their seats, as they all watched the bride walk down the aisle with her father in tow, wearing an extravagant white wedding dress that captured her beauty.

Everyone sat down once it was clear the train full of people were all together. After the couple said their heartfelt vows, the husband planted a soft kiss on his wife's face, while the crowd clapped and cheered. The wedding reception was next as everyone sauntered after the bride to where it would be held. Appetizers were passed all around as people had pleasant conversations with one another. Maddie sat with her family and

Charlotte, enjoying the festivities, and looking at the result of all her hard work. She watched as Miss Caroline investigated the cake with a critical eye, looking out for any imperfections.

"I'm so proud of you, sweetie." Maddie turned to her mom, who looked at her with a sense of pride. Her mom was dressed in an elegant black dress while her black, wavy hair went all the way to her shoulders, the style complimenting her round face.

"Mhmm," Maddie said, a glazed look in her eyes. Her stomach churned with worry as Miss Caroline continued to critique the result of her hard work.

"Everything alright, sweetie?" Maddie turned to her mom, who looked at her with concern.

"Yeah, it's just the way Miss Caroline is judging the wedding cake. I'm a bit scared that she won't like it."

"Well, if she doesn't, I'd say she's a damn fool." A voice chimed in.

Maddie turned around to see Justin in a black suit and tie, looking as handsome as ever. *Did he always look this good?* "Hey Justin, the wedding ceremony was beautiful. Tell your aunt that I said thanks for inviting my family and me."

"Not a problem. You were one of the people who were at the top of my aunt's list, so it was only natural to invite the person who helped make the wedding a big success in the first place."

Maddie looked down at the ground, the compliment having caught her off guard. "Thanks, Justin. That's sweet of you to say." She took in his appearance. "You look handsome."

"Thanks, you look–" Maddie watched as Justin trailed her up and down, admiring the way the dress hugged her figure. He looked down at her shoes, which complimented the dress rather well. In all the years of his life, she had never looked more beautiful. He looked back up again, catching Charlotte's smug smile from behind her. She snapped her fingers in front of him. "Dude, you do know her eyes are up here, right?"

Justin cleared his throat, his mouth suddenly dry and in need of a cold drink. "I–um–I knew that."

"Right... then tell me why you were looking at Maddie as if she were the *only* source of water you would find in an oasis."

He coughed, struggling to answer. He needed a drink and fast—anything to avoid answering this evasive and awkward question. Justin quickly walked away, excusing himself from the girl he had grown to admire.

Maddie frowned and quickly turned to Charlotte. "Did I say anything wrong?" her eyes trailed toward Justin, who quickly excused himself to go get a drink from the table that held the food and drinks.

Charlotte snickered. "Don't worry about him. He's just tongue-tied from seeing you in this gorgeous dress."

Maddie hid her face behind her hair, wondering if Charlotte was right. The sound of someone tapping a glass caught her attention as Maddie watched Miss Caroline try to get everyone's attention. "Friends, family, and loved ones thank you all for coming to celebrate this joyous occasion with me."

Everyone applauded before the noise came to a pause before Miss Caroline spoke up again. "As many of you know, no party could complete without a cake." Justin looked at Maddie, who proceeded to shrink back under the praise. "Which I made myself, of course. You know how I like extravagant things," Miss Caroline said, with a haughty laugh that seemed to echo across the room.

Everyone cheered, except for a few people, those people being Maddie and her family members, along with Charlotte, Amber, and Justin.

"She knows damn well she didn't make that cake," Charlotte whispered to Amber, who nodded in agreement.

Maddie's mom looked at her family friend in disbelief, her composure becoming more and more restless at the thought of her dearest friend taking credit where it wasn't due.

Her husband stopped her in the nick of time, pulling her arm back. "We have to let our daughter handle this on her own. We raised her right, she'll know what to do."

Her mother took a deep breath in response, "Fine, but that doesn't mean that I have to like it."

Her husband kissed the top of his wife's head. "You're doing well, sweetheart."

His wife laughed, leaning against her husband's shoulder.

It looked like Justin had the same idea as he was about to take a step forward, preparing to give his aunt a piece of his mind, when Maddie softly pulled his arm. "Let me handle this, okay? This is my battle to fight, not yours," she whispered into his ear.

Justin looked at Maddie like a proud parent would, ushering her to go forward. With a deep breath, she headed up to Miss

Caroline, who still had that smug smile on her face. "Miss Caroline, may I speak to you in private, please?" Maddie asked, with an air of respect.

Miss Caroline pulled at the collar of her dress nervously. "Of course, dear." She turned to face her audience. "We'll be right back, everyone. Please help yourself to the food and drinks while you wait."

Maddie led Miss Caroline to a private spot to talk, looking around to make sure they were clear of eavesdroppers nearby. Once she was satisfied, Maddie spoke. "You said you're the one who made the cake, right?"

Miss Caroline stumbled over her words. "Um, yes. That's right, dear."

Maddie tapped her chin. "Then, would you like to tell me which flowers you used for the cake's centerpiece?"

Miss Caroline withered under Maddie's glare, trying to come up with an answer, yet words had failed her.

Maddie proceeded to go on. "I used a bouquet made of Hanoi ranunculus and white gardenias." she leaned toward her ear. "I'm giving you a chance to come clean. Either you tell them, or I will. Your choice."

Miss Caroline sighed. "I understand, Maddie. You must know that it was never my intent to steal your shine or anything. You know how some brides can be. They want all the attention to be on them. I suppose I'm one of them."

Maddie patted her on the back, giving her a hug, which Miss Caroline reciprocated. The two went back to the guests, who were enjoying the reception and all it had to offer. Miss Caroline clinked her glass again, causing everyone to turn their attention to the two. "Hello, everyone. I owe you all an apology. You see, I was so caught up in all the attention that I was given, I took credit for what wasn't my own to begin with. Go on, dear."

Maddie stepped forward, with all eyes on her. She never really liked being the center of attention, but maybe she could make an exception. Just this once.

"Everyone, meet the *real* person who oversaw making the cake and decorating it. Please give a round of applause for Madelyn Jones," Miss Caroline declared.

Everyone clapped and whistled for Maddie, with some people asking whether she had a business card they could hand out to her friends. Luckily, she came prepared. She pulled a few business cards out of her purse, giving them to the people who asked. Soon afterward, everyone walked up to the dance floor, dancing the night away.

Justin and Maddie were in the middle of the dance floor, with Maddie's arms around Justin's neck and Justin's hands around her waist. Everything was as it should be. Well, except for one thing. "So, you finally got the exposure you wanted. I'm surprised you didn't expose my aunt's secret to everyone. I don't know what I would have done in your situation," he commented, making eye contact with her.

"No one deserves to be shamed on their wedding day, not even bridezillas, for that matter," Maddie replied, meeting his gaze.

Justin smiled. "Well, I'm proud of you, Firecracker. You finally got everything you wanted."

Maddie gave him an appreciative look. "I couldn't have done it without you. We make a pretty good team."

He chuckled. "We certainly do, Cupcake."

She bit her lip. Now was her chance. "I've been wondering about something, though."

Justin gave her a lopsided grin. "Oh. And what pray tell would that be?"

Maddie rolled her eyes. "Don't act coy with me, Mister. I've had feelings for you, for what, since I was sixteen." She brushed a strand of hair out of her eyes. "If you don't feel the same, I understand–"

Justin quickly put a finger on her lips. "Can I say something, Cupcake?"

She nodded.

The two were quiet for a moment before he spoke up.

"I've only now realized that I have feelings for you now. I just didn't want to tell you before I was sure." He quickly dipped her, looking at the sparkle in her eyes. "Um, do you mind if I kiss you?"

Maddie laughed. "Please."

The world began to fade way as the two looked at each other in anticipation. Looking into his eyes, Maddie felt her heart beat rapidly inside her chest as he leaned in close until their noses were touching. *Oh my god, this is actually happening!* She tried to calm herself down, but it proved to be pointless as he captured her lips into a kiss.

She smiled into the kiss, feeling his soft lips against her and pulled the collar of his shirt closer to her face, savoring the moment between them. *This was definitely worth the wait.*

The two pulled away as she looked into Justin's eyes and vice versa. She watched as he took a deep breath, reaching into his back pocket. *Wait, was he going to do what she thought he was going to do? They were too young to get married.* "You're not proposing, are you?"

Justin bit his lip, struggling not to laugh. "No, I just wanted to give you this because... well, you already know that I like you." He laughed. "Or maybe the kiss wasn't evidence enough?"

She playfully swatted his shoulder.

He chuckled. "Maybe not now, because we're still in college, but hopefully... soon?"

Maddie nodded. "I'd like that." She gingerly took the box from his hands, opening the box to reveal a golden cupcake necklace with a glittering crystal in the middle of it. She looked up at him. "Justin, you didn't have to, but thank you."

He gestured for her to turn around, getting the necklace from the box and clasping the clip around her neck. "Beautiful," he complimented, admiring how the chain seemed to add to her beauty.

She smiled as she continued to dance with him, looking forward to what the future held for both of them.

Made in the USA
Middletown, DE
17 June 2025